B&T 7.42

Risking Love

Doris Orgel

Risking Love

Dial Books

E. P. DUTTON, INC.

NEW YORK

Published by Dial Books
A Division of E. P. Dutton, Inc.
2 Park Avenue
New York, New York 10016

Published simultaneously in Canada
by Fitzhenry & Whiteside Limited, Toronto

Copyright © 1985 by Doris Orgel

The lines from "somewhere i have never travelled, gladly beyond"
are reprinted from ViVa, poems by E. E. Cummings, by permission
of Liveright Publishing Corporation. Copyright 1931, 1959
by E. E. Cummings. Copyright © 1979, 1973 by The Trustees
for the E. E. Cummings Trust. Copyright © 1979, 1973
by George James Firmage.
Design by Atha Tehon
Printed in the U.S.A.
First edition
C O B E
10 9 8 7 6 5 4 3 2 1
Library of Congress Cataloging in Publication Data
Orgel, Doris. Risking love.
Summary: Eighteen-year-old Dinah Moskowitz
uses therapy to confront her past relationships, especially
those with her divorced parents and with her boyfriend,
in order to move forward into the present.
[1. Psychotherapy—Fiction. 2. Divorce—Fiction.]
I. Title.
PZ7.O632Ri 1984 [Fic] 84-5880
ISBN 0-8037-0131-4

Risking Love

* * * * *

It's Friday afternoon of my first week at Barnard. I sit and wait, on tenterhooks. I just met somebody great!

Actually, I'm sitting on a Leatherette stool in Chock Full o' Nuts on the corner of 116th Street and Broadway, sipping coffee. (Dark, with a drop of real milk, please, hold the mello-ream.)

This place is like a fishbowl. Two sides are made of glass. Fish can't see out, though. People in here can. I keep a steady watch. I face the back wall, which is partly mirrored, to seem less obvious about it.

Come on, mirror, give me a break!

Who'm I kidding?

3

I check the clock on the wall to my left. It says four forty. Two more minutes and I'll leave.

I check myself in the mirror. The mirror tells me, Hike that shoulder down. My left one. It has a way of hunching itself up to around ear level whenever I feel nervous, or generally not too great about myself. The rest's okay, fine—looks aren't my problem. I flick my hair behind my ears, smooth it down over my back. It's so light brown, it almost qualifies as blond. I washed it this morning. It's what he'll see of me first. I mean, *would* see . . . I mean, won't . . .

Won't. And the chances are infinitesimal of running into him, just by accident someday, somewhere in the large and teeming campuses of Columbia and Barnard.

Ridiculous to sit here longer. I'm sliding down into a hole.

In this hole—familiar territory—all that I supposedly have going for me, looks, interests, intelligence, don't count. To have strolled down College Walk with this fantastic guy, for all the world as if we two were going somewhere together, also doesn't count, was clearly just a fluke. In this hole I feel pathetic, a nobody that nobody'd come looking for. I think of the big, happy-making things of life, things everyone supposedly gets a crack at. And down in this hole I know those things will pass me by.

We were coming from Zankow's English 370x, Twentieth-Century Poets. It's an advanced course. I think I was the only freshman in it. But my adviser, Mrs. Donadio, thought I should try it. She knows my taste in

4

poetry. In fact, she and I have the same favorite poet, Isabelle Markson. And Zankow thinks highly of Markson's work and is sure to include it in the course, Mrs. Donadio thought.

He looked tweedy and rumpled in a typically academic way. He has an impressive, vaulting forehead, bushy reddish eyebrows, a twitch in one cheek, and his voice is very versatile. He can sound as soulful as an oboe one moment, snide and razor-sharp the next.

He started right in, no introduction, spontaneous, as if the words were his, he the poet of them: "somewhere i have never travelled . . ."

All the little hairs on my arms rose up. Sunlight streamed in through the tall, arched windows. Out there leaves floated around in a dreamy air ballet. I felt as if I were floating with them, light, exhilarated. Like the first time I read this poem, back in grade school, in some anthology. It was a revelation—hey, poems didn't have to rhyme, could have weird punctuation, could knock down all the rules, could reach inside you, "skilfully, mysteriously" stir things around, and thrill you through and through.

This happened to me all over again, until the line "my life will shut very beautifully . . ." That line always loses me. I don't see how one's life shutting could be anything but awful. At that line I returned to there-and-then, looked around the lecture room, at faces, profiles, backs of heads. . . . At one particular back of the head: brown, soft-looking hair, the sun made fiery lights in it. It straggled down over a green-and-blue plaid shirt collar, which was just a little frayed. There's a line in

5

the poem: "your slightest look easily will unclose me."
I repeated it to myself, willing that head to turn around.

Zankow asked, "Does anybody know who wrote that poem?"

Hands went up.

"You tell us." Encouraging smile. "Yes, you in the red turtleneck sweater."

I stood. I said, "e. e. cummings. Small *e*'s, small *c*."

The guy I'd willed to turn around did so. He had gray eyes, set wide apart and deep.

The person behind me had to tap me on the shoulder before I realized Zankow was talking to me. "I *said,* 'Would you care to give us your reaction?' "

"To the poem?" I asked in a daze.

"Yes, to the poem."

"I think it's great."

"How so? Can you elaborate?"

"It's, um, well, expressive. It's surprising." As was the guy's gaze—bright, as if sunlit from the inside—still on me. "It's . . . I don't know . . . it just knocks me out."

"How does it knock you out?"

"By being unconventional. Like, the punctuation: no capital letters, not even spaces between some of the words, just commas. It looks as if . . ."

"Yes? How does it look?"

"As if cummings thumbed his nose at the regular ways of doing things."

"It *looks* that way," said Zankow. "No, don't sit down yet." He wrote *e. e. cummings* on the board. "How does that look to you?"

6

I said, "Modest. As though he didn't want to make a big fuss about himself."

"All right, thank you. Now you may sit down. Are there any other opinions?" He nodded to someone in the second row, who said cummings wrote his name like that so people would notice right away that he was different.

"In other words, to call attention to himself," said Zankow. "*I'd* call that *im*modest. Gimmicky. Ditto the punctuation. See for yourselves." He got two volunteers to copy the first two stanzas on the board:

somewhere i have never travelled,gladly beyond
any experience,your eyes have their silence:
in your most frail gesture are things which enclose me,
or which i cannot touch because they are too near

your slightest look easily will unclose me
though i have closed myself as fingers,
you open always petal by petal myself as Spring opens
(touching skilfully,mysteriously)her first rose

"Thank you," said Zankow. "Now, let's see, what's this poem actually about?"

People said love, roses, springtime.

"Right. The standard, worn-out subjects. Nothing too surprising here. Begging the pardon of the young woman whom it 'knocks out,' I say it's a sham. Dull stuff behind the gimmicks."

The guy two rows in front sent me a look of sympathy.

Zankow went on. "Listen to the ending: 'the voice of your eyes is deeper than all roses)/ nobody,not even the rain, has such small hands.' " He read it coyly and got laughs.

"Since when does rain have hands? And why should hands be small?" He held out his: big meaty chunks. He marched up and down, showing his sausage-shaped fingers. He asked a smashing-looking big, tall woman in the front row, "Would you kindly show us your hands?"

They were extra large.

"Lovely; thank you so much. Small hands were fine for medieval maidens with nothing much to do. But in this day and, let us hope, in this dawn of sexual equality, we ought not to wax ecstatic over *small*—implying weak, incapable—hands."

Right on; I couldn't disagree.

He rubbed his own together, pleased with the job he'd done. He said his chief aim in this course would be to teach the difference between the sham and the true. I stopped listening. I needed to test if he'd ruined the poem for me. I repeated the parts I know by heart. Good, it still gave me gooseflesh.

"I"—*(Ah)*—"like that poem too," said the guy with the sea-gray eyes, waiting for me afterward. "I don't believe I care too much for that professor, though," he added in a leisurely, southern way. We started down the stairs—together, as if that were the natural, the only way to go.

Outside Hamilton Hall, in the sunshine, I felt myself start to "unclose"—oh, "easily," just from his slightly crooked-toothed, powerfully charming grin. He has high, romantic cheekbones, a narrow, straight ridge of a nose, a jutting-forward chin with a hint of a groove in it. He

8

said, "I can't"—*(Ah cain't)*—"respect a professor who sets people up to watch them squirm like he did you."

I asked, "Are you an English major? Have you taken lots of poetry courses?"

He's a biology major. He's taken a few poetry courses. He just hasn't found the right one yet. Then he told me, as though people who don't even know each other's names yet tell each other such things all the time, "One time when I was little, walking home through a stretch of pine woods, I heard a skunk sing."

I thought it was the start of some kind of joke. "Oh?" I said flippantly. "What did it sound like?"

"Creature-ish. Chattery. Mysterious. Definitely musical, but not in any key. And you couldn't follow the tune. I hid behind a tree. I stayed real quiet. The skunk was busy scraping mud and leaves up against a stump, maybe for a nest. Singing while he worked. Or maybe it was a she.

"Anyway"—*(inniway)*—"my brother laughed his head off when I told him. He held his nose, pretended all that happened was I got sprayed and didn't know it. My grandpa, though, believed me. He'd heard a skunk sing too, one time. He could sing just like one. I figured he knew just about everything there was to know. But he couldn't tell me what that skunk song was about. And I haven't found out yet, not in any zoology or animal behavior course."

"You think you might, in the right kind of poetry course?"

"I might. I wouldn't in Zankow's."

We agreed: not a chance.

9

We'd cut across the campus and came to College Walk. He asked, "Where are you headed?"

For a moment I thought he meant in my life. Wherever you are, I almost blurted out. "Chock Full o' Nuts," I said.

The people who work here wear name plates. My counterman's name is George. I ask for a doughnut. I don't really want it. It's just to justify that I'm still sitting here. I put down money. He plunks a doughnut down.

We were three quarters of the distance from the Amsterdam Avenue end of the campus to Broadway. Although I didn't know his name yet, I had more of a feeling for the kind of person he seemed to be than I have about some people I've known all my life. I walked as if the pavement under us were clouds; I felt so happy and so lucky that we'd met. Till this skinny other guy, all out of breath from running, grabbed him by the shoulders. "Gray, Gray! I was hoping I'd find you! They called! Right after you left. About Belinda. They want you to call right back."

Gray let out a yell. "Hooray, I knew it!" He turned to me. "Listen—" He didn't know what to call me.

"Dinah."

"Listen, Dinah, I'm really sorry. I have to go make this call. See you later, okay?" And took off like greased lightning toward Ferris Booth, where there are telephones.

"See you later" is just something people say. You're not supposed to take it literally. . . .

The other guy was odd-looking: string-bean–thin; terrible, slouching posture; black hair, curly, almost an Afro; big dark eyes; long, curved nose with a bump near the top. And he wore a grape-colored T-shirt that proclaimed in white letters, *Bird Lives!*

He shifted his weight from one foot to the other. He drew in his breath, watching Gray disappear, shrugged, smiled as if to say, See what the mere mention of Belinda can do? He introduced himself: Joe Morgenthau, Gray's roommate since they were freshmen.

The counter here is glaring red Formica. Have I sat at it so long, it's started to do funny things to my vision? Or is there really a rose, palest pink, lying across my doughnut?

"Hey, thanks for waiting," says Gray.

"Oh, I wasn't waiting, just passing the time." It's such a blatant lie, and I'm so beside-myself glad, I burst out laughing. The rose has a powerful fragrance. I hold it up to his nose.

He breathes it in. Sits down next to me, orders coffee. We introduce ourselves.

His name is Graham Dawson. Kids called him Graham Cracker when he was little. He comes from Naples, Florida.

"Can I ask you something?"
"Shoot."

"Who's Belinda?"

"Well," he says in a tender voice, "she's eleven feet long, weighs twelve hundred and thirty-one pounds; she's dirtyish white all over, with smart little bright blue eyes on either side of her head, and dang intelligent, too."

"The abominable snow woman?"

"Not even close! She's a beluga whale. Down at the New York Aquarium in Brooklyn. And she's pregnant! There have been fewer than ten beluga calves born into captivity anywhere in the world so far," he explains. "She'll need a lot of extra watching." He's had an application in to do research, and now they're taking him on, as a volunteer keeper. It's a tremendous opportunity. Today's his lucky day.

"Say, could I have a glass of water, please?" he asks the counterman.

George says, "This ain't the Plaza Hotel," but obliges.

Instead of drinking from the glass, Gray puts the rose in it.

The minute hand of the clock has been racing. Our coffees have gotten cold. Before I know it, it's ten of six; I'm supposed to be home at six.

Gray dampens some napkins, wraps them around the rose.

We pick up our notebooks, get ready to go. We say, in the same breath, "When will I see you?" And we link little fingers, as you are supposed to, when this happens.

We leave Chock Full o' Nuts, our little fingers still linked. Gray says, "How about ten tomorrow morning?"

One Christmas when he was ten years old, he came up here on a visit. He saw his first snow. And he saw the elephant herd in the Museum of Natural History. They looked so alive, the grown ones' tusks proudly piercing the air and the little ones crowding against their mamas. He almost could hear their hoof treads. He fell in love with them, with the snow, with all of New York City. He thought it was the second-best place he'd ever been to. The first-best place to Gray was, still is, the Everglades.

Anyway, he asks me if I'd like to meet him in the East African Hall of the museum, where those elephants are. Of course I've seen them before, but I want to see them with him. "Great!" I say it so eagerly, I'm suddenly stricken with embarrassment, pull my pinkie away, fumble in my change purse for a quarter.

"Back where Ah come from," he says with an exaggerated drawl, "whoever breaks the pinkie link has to pay the penalty." He lowers his head and our lips touch. The penalty part is, it's over very fast.

There are two pay phones on this corner. I drop a quarter in one.

The traffic light turns green. Gray waves to me. He starts crossing Broadway, facing backward, holding me in his sight.

I dial home. "Dad? I'll be a little late. . . ."

Gray disappears into the campus.

I turn the other way, face west. The Hudson is a dark, glorious blue; wind whips up frothy whitecaps. The sun is a great glowing disk descending over New Jersey. The clouds are turning rose-golden-gorgeous. So is my whole life!

I touch the rose to my cheek. I pity the harried, tired-looking people passing by, for whom nothing glorious is beginning. Then—I've put the receiver back on its hook—a rush of panic starts: What if I'm not up to this, disappoint him, wreck it? West of here the street slopes very steeply downhill. So will my whole, whole life. . . .

*   *   *   *   *

I

Monday, April 4, 3:40–4:30 P.M.

Dr. Schneck is very short. I'm not a giant myself, but feel like one as we shake hands. Maybe she has shrunk I wisecrack, following her through the corridor from the waiting room into here.

This is a corner room with windows to the east and south—great views, I bet. But Levolor blinds shut it out. The blinds, the rug, the furniture, everything except the couch is shades of beige and brown. The effect is hazy, dusky, meant to be soothing, I guess. *If* you're upset, which I'm not.

Dr. Schneck motions me to a chair, brown-upholstered with wooden arms; comfortable, but not too.

15

She sits down opposite me in the same kind of chair and says, with a trace of an accent, "Tell me about yourself."

"My name is Dinah Moskowitz. I'm eighteen years old. My life is just fine. I'm a freshman at Barnard. I do well at school." *Did*. Right now, I'm not doing so great in a couple of my courses. "I have friends, um, a boyfriend." I don't like that word. Why not *lover*? Because this doctor is so old, and would be shocked? Anyway, I conjure him to mind, let my fingers meander through the soft curly hair like fine brown fur across his chest. "Nothing's wrong with me. I'm normal, no problems."

Dr. Schneck smiles. She has a big, wide mouth for such a little face. She's probably wondering what am I doing here?

"I promised my father I'd see you."

The smile seems friendly. As well it should, at sixty-five dollars for fifty minutes! How much does that come to per smile?

"How does this work, exactly? I mean, for people *with* problems?"

"They talk; I listen."

Sounds like a gyp. "Do you give them advice? Tell them what you think they should do?"

"Actually, no; I don't tend to."

Good, fine with me. "So then how does this help? How do people with problems get better?"

"By expressing whatever they think of and feel as freely as they can. By starting to listen to themselves in new ways."

Hmm. Sounds vague. I listen to her accent. It's so

slight, she must have been quite young—which it's hard to imagine her ever having been—when she first came to this country from I wonder where.

". . . becoming aware of patterns, piecing together meanings. . . ."

I become aware that her skirt is brown and beige, and her blouse is also beige. Snail colors! Schneck means snail, I remember; like schnecken, snail-shaped cinnamon buns my grandmother used to make. Snails can pull into their shells; how convenient! "I hope you won't think this is rude, but it sounds to me as if the people who come here with problems have to do all the work themselves."

"Much of it, yes. Though I can sometimes help by pointing out ways in which things they tell me are connected."

It doesn't sound worth the money. True, Dad's friend Bill Hammond was in an awful mess and got better. On the other hand, my friend Julie Warshkower has gone from shrink to shrink for years and isn't any happier, and still has a huge inferiority complex. Her next-to-last shrink put her on a diet. Her current shrink serves coffee and cookies. . . . "What sort of things do people talk about?"

"Whatever they want. Whatever they're thinking about."

"I wouldn't know where to start. My thoughts are veering in eighty-seven directions." She wears a wide gold wedding band. Is Schneck her married or her maiden name? *Maiden;* what an old-fashioned word. Was the name once Schneckenhausen, Schneckenberg, or Scheckenheim? Did some lazy U.S. immigration official lop it off so he wouldn't have to spell the whole thing out? This nearly happened to my great-grandfather Moskowitz, except he was stubborn, yelled "No, no, no," the one word of English he already knew, till the immigration official gave in and spelled out the whole name on the form. It's ironic that Dad now uses Moss as his stage and TV name. Whereas Mom's still Mrs. Moskowitz. . . .

"Would you like to tell me any of the eighty-seven directions?"

"Mainly I'm thinking I'm wasting your time."

She pushes her horn-rimmed glasses up into her hair and asks, "Are you also thinking that I am wasting yours?"

Absolutely. She hit the nail on the head. I could be at Gray's. We could be "practicing." On his Futon. Under the panther, eagle, osprey, manatee, and alligator posters. Kind of like Adam and Eve. Except *they* didn't need to practice. . . .

Dr. Schneck is waiting for an answer to her question. But how do you say to an older person—highly trained and highly paid—Yes, I think you are wasting my time?

I flip my hair forward. I braided it into a single braid for a change. I flip it to the side, curl the ends around my finger.

Hers is dark brown, almost black. Not dyed. Very little gray in it, just at the sides; surprising. "You have nice hair," I say. She wears it swept back from her forehead, turned under. Her hairline is perfect. Her forehead's not as wrinkled as the rest of her face. Boy, is she old.

All this time she's been looking straight at me. She's used to looking at people head-on, it doesn't faze her. It does me. I can't look directly back for longer than a second at a time.

I look around. Along the wall across from me are bookshelves, floor to ceiling. In front of the east windows is a plant stand with African violets, ferns, begonias, and an avocado plant, spindly and tall. In third grade, in Rowayton, our class grew avocados from pits, suspended on toothpicks over glasses of water. "I hate avocados." I hadn't planned on saying that. "Sorry; that sounds rude. I didn't mean your plant."

"In this room it is all right to sound rude, or however you feel. What *did* you mean?"

"I don't know, exactly."

"Try inexactly then." She looks as if this really interests her.

"Okay, well, it's an ugly color. We had this big monstrosity in our kitchen in Rowayton, an avocado-green Coldspot refrigerator. It's still there." Uh-oh, help! Get me off this subject! If I had the courage, I'd pry two slats in those blinds apart and see what's out there. I wonder what she thinks of me. And I think about Mom. That's supposed to happen, isn't it, when the shrink's a woman, with the same color eyes, avocado-green?

"Do you want to hear about my childhood? It was normal, nothing much to tell. I was born in Rowayton, Connecticut. I lived there till I was almost twelve. No brothers or sisters, no hang-ups about that. And I get along with both my parents. I have good, grown-up relationships with them."

As a color for eyes, avocado-green's okay. I think about that, and a dress Mom used to have that color. It was silk, or taffeta. It rustled when she moved. And her hair piled on top of her head, like a crown. Back then she fussed more with her clothes and hairdos. Only the hairdo is collapsing, one side falling down as she leans against the Coldspot, Dad—I thought it was Dad!—leaning up against her. Even though Dad's not that tall, and didn't have spiky gray hair sticking up like porcupine quills. . . .

Dr. Schneck goes "Ahem" softly. "You were saying?"

"It doesn't matter." I muster up the courage, stand, push two thin brown slats apart. There, to the south, is the Empire State Building, antenna glinting in the sun. What a shame to shut it out. I'd like to yank the damn blinds up. "Look," I say, not looking at her, "I came here because I promised my father I'd discuss this one thing: Next year. I'm taking next year off from school."

I think of the afternoon the acceptance came. I was so thrilled! And relieved, that I wouldn't have to move away, into some dingy dorm room at Smith or Vassar, my two other choices. I went out on the terrace. There was Julie, at her window just across the avenue, waving *her* letter; she's gotten in to Barnard too. That evening Dad took us to Pinocchio's to celebrate, just him and me and Julie. Pat, the woman in his life before Audrey, was out of town, which made it even better.

Dr. Schneck asks, "What are you planning to do next year?"

"Well, you see, my, um, friend, Gray, has this fabulous job lined up, as assistant park ranger in the Everglades, in Florida. He comes from near there. It's his favorite place in the world."

"And you?"

"I'm going too!"

"And do what?"

"I don't know; find a job, study on my own. That isn't the point."

"Tell me what the point is."

I tell her how endangered the Everglades and its many species of rare animals are, by drought, fires, wildlife poachers, and what the park rangers do about it.

"Yes, but what will *you* do there?"

Why is everybody I've told this to so dense on the subject? "Whatever I do will be just as important as what I'd be doing as a Barnard sophomore."

"Which would be?"

"Oh, taking *Beowulf,* or Chaucer, wondering if the world needs another English major." I lean forward. "Don't you see?"

She leans toward me. "I can see that you want to be near your friend." She sits back, clasps her hands together loosely, palms open. "Tell me more about it."

"It's not that complicated!" I say, exasperated.

Even Gray brought up worries, about unimportant things like if we'd have a place to live with enough privacy, and if we'd need to pretend we were married.

And Julie—she's known me forever, since seventh grade—was bowled over, "Wow! You really, really love him, right?" We were on our way home, waiting at Madison and Eighty-sixth Street. I didn't like being asked that. I dashed across. "Hey," she yelled, "the light's still red!"

A taxi had to slam on its brakes. A truck stopped short to let me by.

"Did I say something wrong?" she asked when she finally caught up to me.

"No, just forget it."

I say to this psychiatrist: "It's really very simple. . . ." If I'm not with him, I lose him!

She asks me, "Simple, how?"

"We need to be together. That's the most important thing. You may think people of my generation just casually hop in and out of each other's, um, lives. Well, not us. We didn't, um . . ." How did I get onto this? I don't have to tell her!

"Didn't what?"

"Oh, rush into anything we didn't mean. What I'm trying to say, if you can believe this, is that I was"—I use the antiquated word—"a virgin."

Till the night after Thanksgiving. It was supposed to be a gala event. I'd brought a bottle of Dad's good Pinot Chardonnay—he gladly gave me one, not knowing the occasion. We played music: Gray's old record of Brahms's Second; Beatle albums; a tape Joe'd put together of Ellington, Thelonious Monk, Hines, and other jazz greats. We took our time, tried to get very relaxed. The familiar, nonfeatured things felt as wonderful as ever: Tracing the rim of his ear with my tongue. Fitting my lips to the ridge of his nose. Touching each other's eyelids. To the fingers and the lips, eyelids feel like flower petals. "Unclosing," like in the poem. At least, starting to . . .

"You know what?" he said into my ear, fitting his body to mine. "Maybe that skunk in the woods that day sang about making love. What do you think, Dinah? Hey, that tastes salty. You cryin'? What about?"

Him saying it, so straight and simply. Me not getting it past my lips. Not even "afterward."

I needed to take lots of breaks. One time, to cheer ourselves on, we sang along with Paulie, Ringo, George, and the late great John Lennon. "Hard day's night" was right; the lyrics fit too well. Gray truly was "working like a dog." Why couldn't I open "petal by petal," like in the cummings poem? It damn near took a battering ram. Gray was sweating. I felt sorry for him. For me, too. I had that medieval thing, a hymen, supposedly a thin little membrane. Mine felt more like a brick wall.

It hurt. I got tenser. It hurt even more. After the I-forget-how-manieth try, Gray went into Joe's room to see if Joe had any pot left from the last time he'd tried quitting cigarettes. Yes, enough for one meager joint. And we smoked it. We hadn't planned to. We'd thought the high of sex would exceed an ordinary, pot-induced one.

When it was finally "afterward" (in some novels I've

read, that word is supposed to imply that the sex was superb, with tidal-wave orgasms and monumental bliss), Gray said that giving ourselves to each other, as we'd done, was special and rare, meant more than the greatest pleasure and excitement, and not to worry, those would come with practice. He felt good. "I love you," he said, kissed me, and fell asleep like a rock.

I went into the bathroom. I washed away the blood, etc. I had Gray's ratty old rust-color bathrobe on that had passed down to him from his brother. I had rings under my eyes; my hair was matted together. When I came out of the bathroom, the front door opened; Joe was home. And even though it was four in the morning, and I'd never been there so late, or so early, Joe gallantly seemed unsurprised. Awful as I looked, he said, "Hey, Dynamite." He always calls me that. Not in a flirting way.

He'd planned to spend the weekend at his girl friend Carole's house. Well, they'd had a "disagreement." He apologized for barging in at such an hour.

"Joe, don't apologize; you live here!" I said in a shaky voice.

"Hey, you're shivering." He put his arm around me. In an entirely brotherly way. "This place is as cold as a barn." His hand lay lightly on the bathrobe sleeve, barely touching it, much less me. Yet sparks shot through. What was happening? Was this an unforeseen side effect of Gray's opening-up-of-me labors? I gave Joe a panic-stricken look and bolted down the hall.

Gray was sleeping on his side. I fitted myself to him so that we were as tight as spoons. I lay there disliking,

24

distrusting myself, thinking how different this night had turned out from how I'd imagined. Frankly, longing for my own bed.

Dr. Schneck says, "Yes?"

Thank God I'm not a patient of hers and don't have to tell this. I ask her, "Do you have any patients my age?"

"Some." And she adds, although I didn't ask, "They do find it possible, old though I am, to talk to me about sex."

Well, good for them. I return to the subject I'm here to discuss: "Next year's all decided. I can go back to college later, re-enroll anytime, it's really not a problem. The one who has a problem with it is my father."

We had this dumb, hurtful fight about it. We were in the kitchen, cleaning up. The Hammonds, Audrey Gerstein, the current love of Dad's life, and Gray had been over to dinner. Dad said, "That boy of yours was pretty quiet. Is 'The environment' the only topic that gets a rise out of him?"

"*A*, Dad, he's not a 'boy.' *B*, you're just miffed because he never heard of 'Swish-O, the magic cleansing powder' Audrey's doing the ad campaign for. Well, he and Joe don't happen to own a TV. And, *C*, yes, it so happens other things 'get a rise out of him.'" I felt myself flush at the wording.

Dad turned red too. He made a big clatter, scraping the plates.

"Gray cares about all sorts of things. He likes to listen

to music, go to the movies, read books, go to plays. You'd be surprised. A lot of the same things you cared about."

My father said, "Care*d*? You think I don't anymore?"

"Well, it's just that Whooshies"—*(Your baby's tush deserves a Whooshy; Whooshies are soft as the breeze)*— "and your other important voice-overs take up so much of your time."

Maybe I'd had too much wine. I hadn't meant to be that rough on Dad. Once I got going, though, I couldn't stop. If I could just have mentioned that Gray thinks a lot of Dad, really, and was mainly just shy at the dinner, I could have saved us the rest of the scene. I could have saved Dad sixty-five bucks. And I wouldn't be sitting here now, brooding about it.

"He cares a lot about *me*," I went on. "And it's very, very mutual."

"Honey, remember: You are very, very young."

Dad's forty-eight. Not that you'd guess. He runs around the reservoir most mornings, plays tennis, keeps trim. He looks forty, tops. And can *sound* in his teens, can make his voice crack and go falsetto, as if it hadn't settled into its permanent register yet.

"You and Mom were just as young. At least Mom was. Remember?"

"Ouch. I thought you and I had a pact."

Right, not to discuss him and Mom. They "eloped." Mom didn't even finish out the school year. They didn't tell their parents till afterward.

"Don't worry, Dad, we're not about to follow your example!"

He doubled over with theatrical pain, making believe I'd punched him where it hurt the most.

"Cut it out, Dad. Don't you know when I'm being serious?" And I told him our plan for next year.

He'd just flicked a pat of butter off a plate. Now he ran his fingers, with butter all over them, through his styled-to-look-casual hair. "Dinah, you don't need to do this to yourself."

"What do you mean?"

"I mean, banish yourself to some miserable mosquito swamp, just because you've been to bed with the guy!"

I slammed the dishwasher shut. I wiped my sopping hands on my expensive silk trousers and walked out of the kitchen.

Dad came after me. "Sorry, I shouldn't have said that. Dinah, listen, just do me one favor. . . ."

"My father asked me, as a favor to him, to come and talk to you about next year. My father has great confidence in you, on account of Bill Hammond, who says that seeing you helped him a lot. So here I am. But as I said, I've already made up my mind."

Dr. Schneck breathes in deeply. It makes a kind of raspy sound. The next moment she starts to get out of her chair.

I stand up too—demolished. It isn't time yet! Whoever heard of a psychiatrist sending a person away ten minutes early?

She reaches for a Kleenex from a box on her desk. To my huge relief, she sits back down. And blows her nose.

I sit down again too.

"I have a slight allergy, always at this time of year. Tell me, why did *you* stand up?"

"I thought you wanted me to leave."

"Why? The session is not over yet."

"I know, but I thought you thought, if my mind is that made up, there's nothing more to talk about."

"You looked very sad while you were thinking that."

"I did? Well, I was. I felt awful."

"Why?"

"Wouldn't anyone?"

She leans forward in her chair. She says, in a tone of wanting me to get this, "We are not concerned with what 'anyone' would feel. *You* felt awful, thinking I wanted you to leave. What occurs to you about that?"

Tears are occurring behind my eyes. My mind feels muddy. Like the frog pond in our yard in Rowayton when I poked around in it with a stick, and muck floated up from the bottom. "Nothing. Except, I . . ."

"Except?"

"I guess I didn't want to leave yet."

"Good." She sits back, crosses her legs.

I sit back. My face, which has been burning hot, feels a little cooler. The muck in the pond in my mind starts to settle. "I guess I do have some problems."

"Yes? Can you tell me about them?"

"I get pretty blue sometimes. Even when things are going fine. Especially then. I get scared I'll mess them up. Or that I already did."

"What things, for instance?"

For instance, my whole life. I shrug. "I can't really say."

"Perhaps you will be able to when you feel you know me better."

It's 4:29 and a half. When will that be?

She leafs through her appointment book. "Would you like to talk some more, another time?"

"Yes."

She offers me Thursday, at twenty past four.

Fine. I don't have a class then. If I did, I'd cut it.

II

Thursday, April 7, 4:20–5:10 P.M.

"How are you feeling today?"

She's wearing the same skirt as last time, a brown silk tailored blouse, and her shoes are bone.

"Good, I felt good. I was looking forward to coming here. Then these two brats got on the elevator. They really annoyed me. One of them was trying to blow the world's biggest artificial grape-flavored purple bubble-gum bubble. One bubble exploded all over her face. While she was picking it off she said, not even bothering to whisper, 'I bet *she* gets off at eighteen. You know whose floor that is.' "

I don't like how I sound, bratty myself. "It's a dumb

thing to start talking about, don't you think? Should I have started where I left off the last time?"

Dr. Schneck says, "It was fine to start just as you did. The only 'should' is to express, as directly as you can, what goes through your mind. And through the rest of you. Feel free to mention bodily sensations too." As if it showed! I have a peculiar taste in my mouth, not of food or gum; I don't know what of.

"Don't worry in what order you say things, or whether they sound polite. Just let yourself talk."

"Okay. There's this taste in my mouth. I don't know what it is. I stopped at Baskin-Robbins on my way here. I had a Pralines 'n' Cream ice cream cone. That's not it. I walked all the way here from school. Usually on Thursdays my friend Julie Warshkower and I walk home together. Today I wanted to be by myself to think about coming here, what to talk about. The park was beautiful, all the magnolias and cherries in bloom. It was like a spring day in Rowayton, going to my treehouse in the woods behind our house. It was my private place. . . ." In spite of what she said about talking freely, I feel foolish, like I'm wasting time, bringing up this bit of nostalgia. And I get mad all over again at those kids in the elevator. "The other little brat in the elevator said, 'Yeah, she guessed I'd get off on your floor too.' And she stuck a big hank of hair in her mouth, chewed on it. Yecch. . . ." A bratty sound. *Now* what should I say?

"Funny, with all the sketching out I did, I can't think of any topic. I just feel so embarrassed!"

"What about?"

"That I'm here. That it shows so much, those little girls could tell." I swallow. "I still have that taste in my mouth."

"Can you describe it?"

"It's not a taste, exactly. It's just there. No, I can't." Now I feel dumb, like I'm failing at this. Quick, I need a subject I can sound my age, coherent, about.

Gray, how smart and wonderful he is. I can be very coherent on the subject. I make it clear as the sunlight outside these Levolors that having Gray in my life proves I'm not the obvious mess and nutcase those kids in the elevator took me for.

"My friend Julie says, if she'd met him first, she'd have given up Milky Ways and Mars bars, her two major vices, for good, on the merest chance of his giving her a tumble.

"Mom, who was never bowled over by anyone I've dated, really likes him. I think she's kind of surprised that someone so purposeful and grown-up is seriously interested in me.

"Dad's the only holdout. Even Audrey Gerstein, with her myopic Madison Avenue outlook, can't help liking Gray.

"Yesterday, at the aquarium . . ." I tell how he got down in the whale pool and played with Belinda. I feel good talking about this. I figure Dr. Schneck doesn't get to hear about pregnant whales every day.

She listens with concentration.

"When will *you* say something?"

She answers imperturbably, "When I feel that something needs saying."

I tell how Gray and I met. What Zankow did to me with that poem. I ask, "Do you know it, by any chance?" and, quickly, avert my eyes.

Hey, the rug isn't just beige. It has an intricate weave of orange, maize, and blue in it. And Dr. Schneck's little shoes, size five at the most, are delicate, with narrow T-straps that make her instep look graceful. And her legs are shapely.

She says, "Why do you look away?"

Because too much depends on what I asked. I wish I could take it back. On the one hand, I'd hate to see her looking blank if she never heard of that poem. On the other hand, I'd feel funny if she felt some particular way about it and it showed. I know this sounds crazy. I'm too ashamed to mention it. So I say, "I guess I'm just not used to staring straight at people's faces," and let it go at that. And look at her, to prove I can.

She says, "I do know the poem."

Hello again, rug. Hi there, my slightly beat-up blue running shoes, size seven and a half. Staring down in silence, I almost hear the seconds ticking by.

"Do other people sit here and not talk?" Oops. I forgot; other people are out.

I grope in my canvas shoulder bag, find a pack of Velamints, pop one in my mouth, feel rude, start to offer her one, know she won't take it, pull back, put on a little self-conscious smile.

"You must be wondering why I wanted to come back —I really did! And now I'm wasting this whole session." I have a sharp premonition of how awful I will feel when it's over.

33

She looks at me placidly, yet expectantly, and opens her hands in her lap. The gesture says there's plenty of time.

I try for a casual conversational tone. "How long, would you say, psychotherapy takes, on the average?"

"There really is no 'average.' It depends on the person. Her reasons for coming. What she hopes to achieve. How ready she is for this process, which, I think you already realize, is in many ways not easy. And it depends very much on how well the particular patient and therapist work together."

"Well, how long, would you think, it would take for someone like me?"

She sticks her glasses up in her hair, leans toward me. "There is no one like you. I don't say this teasingly. You are an individual, which is to say, unique. I'd have to know a lot more about you before I could venture a guess."

"Oh, well, it doesn't matter. The most time I could give it would be till May nineteenth."

"What happens on May nineteenth?"

"I'm going to London with Dad. He has a small part in a movie there. Depending on when he finishes, we may drive around the countryside for a week or so. I'm looking forward to it. . . ."

I wait for her to say something, ask me something.

I shove my hands, my fists, actually, into my blue-denim shirt pockets. I tell the Levolors what a great trip it'll be.

I keep waiting, pretty hard.

34

"We'll be back on June ninth. On the twelfth, I have to be up at Silverbirch for a refresher course in senior lifesaving. Because they offered me the job of assistant-head waterfront counselor. It's kind of an honor. I'm excited about it." Meantime my right fist has been digging so hard into my pocket, the pocket seam's starting to give. I take out my hand, play with a strand of my hair, catch myself about to stick it in my mouth; what was I going to do, suck on it? Hey, *that* was it. My stomach lurches—bodily sensation; should I tell it?

She's been sitting with her finger to her chin, like *The Thinker* by Rodin (full-page illustration in my Art History text). She asks, "Did you want me to ask you to keep on coming to see me until the nineteenth of May?"

I nod. I feel incredibly foolish.

She sits back. "Let me say why I'd prefer to plan on two more sessions for now, and then see where we are."

My premonition of feeling awful comes true ahead of time. I ask her, "Why?" It comes out like a dirge, a lament.

"It's fairer to you. You will know better if you want to continue. And if so, whether with me. Meantime, we can get to know each other better."

Each other? Who's she kidding?

"How do you feel about that?"

"Fine."

"You seem bothered. Won't you face me?"

I do.

"What bothers you? Won't you try and say?"

"*We*. Getting to know *each other*. How's that going to happen, with me doing all the talking?"

She opens her hands in her lap again, so relaxed! "You will see. You will get more of a sense of whether I'm the sort of person who can understand you, whom you can trust. This is important in determining if we can work together well."

I tune out. A hank of hair's in my mouth, ugh, disgusting, I don't care. I'm thinking of standing up to my shoulders in clumps of jewelweed, in the woods behind our house, my first morning back from camp. Its flame-colored blossoms, shaped like little trumpets, its fat ripe green pods ready to burst. Chewing fiercely on the ends of my braids, bursting the pods, fast, fast, burst them all, before Mom called me in. . . .

"You seem quite far away," says Dr. Schneck. "What are you thinking about?"

"Jewelweed."

"What is jewelweed?"

Good, see, you don't know everything. . . . "Oh, just a weed. Big tall stalks, little blossoms, yellowish-orange . . ." The color of egg yolks congealing on my breakfast plate. I get nauseous, almost belch out loud.

"What were you thinking about jewelweed?"

"Nothing! I just thought of it, that's all."

"You sound angry. Are you angry with me?"

Typical! I've heard and I've read that psychiatrists think you feel all sorts of big emotions toward them. That is so conceited, when they're really nobody to you!

I don't need to look at my watch. I know the session's over.

36

She says, "Shall we schedule two more sessions then, for now? I have the same two times available next week. You may want to talk it over with your father first, and call me. I answer the telephone myself between twelve and one. Any other time, you can leave a message with my service."

"I don't have to talk it over with Dad; he'll agree. It's okay," I say grudgingly.

"See you Monday, then, at three forty." She grasps the chair arms, is about to stand.

I beat her to it, leap to my feet, rush out.

III

Monday, April 11, 3:40–4:30 P.M.

I press the buzzer to 18E.

What garish wallpaper out here! An interior decorator's notion of tendrils and blossoms, not like anything in nature.

I press again.

Touch-me-not's another name for jewelweed. If you pick the pods when they're good and ripe, they squiggle up in your hand, as if they were begging No, please, please, don't burst me. . . .

Hey, what's taking her so long?

I buzz again. Did I make a mistake? Is it the wrong day? The wrong time?

I check today's *Spectator;* it's Monday all right. I hold my watch to my ear. It's ticking. Three forty, just as she said.

Do psychiatrists get called away to emergencies? She'd have left word with the doorman. Could *she* be having an emergency? What if she's lying in there on the floor, her little bone shoes pointing up? What if she had a heart attack or something? *My* heart drums, rat, tat, tat. My middle finger jabs the buzzer and presses, so hard the blood drains from under the fingernail; the fingernail turns white. Meantime my other nails are digging into the flesh of my hand.

There, at last—the buzzing back. I clutch the door-knob, turn it, enter.

Last week, both times, I sat out in the waiting room for a couple of minutes. First the patient before me came out. Thursday a youngish woman who kept her eyes to the floor. Monday a man, middle-aged, with a briefcase. When they'd left, Dr. Schneck came out and asked me in.

This time she's already in the waiting room. She looks perfectly all right, color in her cheeks. She says, "I'm sorry I kept you waiting. I was in another room; I didn't hear the buzzer right away."

Of course, simple explanation! This isn't just an office suite, it's a whole apartment. She could have been in the kitchen, running the water, or using the toilet, her private one, or had a radio on somewhere, too loud.

"If it happens again, please do just as you did, keep on ringing until I ring back, all right?" she says good-humoredly.

Not all right! It better not happen again! The inside of my hand's still raw where my fingernails dug in. "I was really worried. I thought something might have happened to you. . . ."

"Yes?"

By now we're in our chairs, as usual. She moves forward in hers, interested. "What did you think might have happened to me?"

"Oh, that you weren't feeling well. . . ."

She's not even wearing the bone shoes, but a sturdy-looking pair of navy blue ones. "How 'not well'?"

I don't care how badly she wants to know, or that this is not a social situation. It's wrong to mention heart attack to somebody her age. I shift around in my chair, change the subject. "It feels like ages since the last time I was here."

She adjusts her glasses on her nose. "Why do you think that is?"

"Oh, I guess because a lot of things came up in the meantime."

"Such as?"

"Such as, a big account Dad was sure he'd get fell through. Some status-y computer commercials. It would have paid lots of money. But he's more upset that it could mean he's slipping. He and Audrey had these soul-searching talks about whether Whooshy disposable diapers have 'trivialized his image.'

"Audrey said definitely not. Then she dropped a hint —thud! She wants to come to London with us. She batted her long eyelashes, made of the finest ermine hair, and wheedled, 'Nicky, please!'

"She'd spoil the whole trip. She and I'd be stuck together the whole time Dad would be working. If she comes . . ."

"Yes? What?"

Nothing. I'll stay home. I don't say this out loud. I tell about something else:

"Friday night Joe's uncle, Lucky, played at the West End. That's a bar up near school where they have live jazz. With a pretty well-known bass player, Chester Baron. Lucky is a terrific pianist, but not too well-known anymore, and hasn't played anywhere in quite a while. I don't know if I told you, Joe is kind of a jazz nut. He has his own show on the Columbia radio station. And he was the one who gave the manager at the West End the idea of Lucky and Chester playing there. So he was really excited about it. Carole, his girl friend, whom he's been fighting with, was supposed to come in from Vassar and go with us. Of all times to stand him up! Wait till you hear the excuse: She had to dog-sit. She lives in a dorm where they allow pets, and her roommate went away for the weekend, and the roommate's poodle doesn't like being alone. Joe was crushed. He tried not to show it. He went through almost a whole pack of Marlboros—regulars, not even lights. Even though he'd quit. I feel as if I'm rambling."

"Don't worry about it. Keep on."

"Okay. Yesterday Gray and I were supposed to go to Mom's. But then Gray got a call from Phil d'Alessandro, the beluga whales' keeper. Phil had somewhere urgent to go and asked Gray could he come down and spell him. Gray said sure. He was glad to have an excuse to go down and check on Belinda. The last time he saw her she had seemed not quite her chirpy self.

"I said, Of course, I understood. I thought I'd go to Mom's by myself. But then Julie came by with some Renaissance slides to review for an Art History quiz. By the time we got done with them, it was too late. I called Mom. She said, 'Okay, come next week.'

"In the evening Gray came over. Dad and Audrey were out. And we, um . . ."

Practiced. Just between me and me, it was not great. My room's too ruffled and little-girlish. Those four angel faces by Sir Joshua Reynolds over my bed didn't help either, looking down all benign and innocent. And the diaphragm's a drag. Filling it with Orthogynol, putting it in—it's like saying, Watch it, sperms, if this gizmo doesn't get you, this glop surely will!

I wished it were last fall again, with the "main event" still off in the future, when every other little fleshly thing we used to do felt so fantastic. Like just putting my face against his cheek, shaved or stubbly, no matter. Like just his fingertips on the underside of my arm, where the skin is pale and secret. Or on my earlobes. Whoever started the rumor that earlobes aren't sensitive was probably in the jewelry business, conning people into having them pierced. Mine are sensitive, all right. More so than other parts of me, rubber-capped, smeared with spermicide. Why hasn't some advertising genius renamed those products, improved their image? But how much difference would it make, standing in the bathroom under cold fluorescent lights, pants down, inserting your Chapeau d'Amour by Yves Saint Laurent,

42

filled with Cupid's Cream by Estée Lauder, or Aphrodi-jel, by Lanvin?

Anyway, last night, with Gray right there close, on top of me, in me, I felt more alone than when I'm alone. The noises of trucks and honking and sirens down on the street didn't abate, or fade altogether, as noise sometimes does. And I couldn't shut my thoughts off. I thought of being here, in this consulting room. And now that I'm here, I think of being there.

"You seem preoccupied," says Dr. Schneck.

Postoccupied. No, not funny, and not fair.

"You started to tell me that your friend Gray came over."

"Right. Well, we . . ." What? Went to bed? Too evasive. Had sex? Too detached. Oh, the hell with it. I straighten up in my chair, level my shoulders. "You know, I really expected to get someplace today. But all I've been doing is rambling on, talking because I'm supposed to, not *about* anything."

Her pointy chin juts forward. "Oh, I disagree."

"You do? What do *you* think I've been talking about?"

"Disappointments: Your father did not get the computer commercials. Audrey wants to come along and spoil your trip to London. Your friend Joe's girlfriend stood him up. Your friend Gray went to the aquarium instead of with you to Rowayton. And later, when he came to visit you, I gather you made love—"

"I didn't call it that!"

"Yes, I noticed. At any rate, it was not all you had hoped?"

Right. She bounces it all back to me. Is that all that

happens here? Then why isn't there a net between us; why aren't we holding paddles in our hands?

She wants to know what I'm thinking about.

"Something *not* disappointing: Ping-Pong." I shake my wrist loose, like I did when I was about to serve. "I used to be pretty good at Ping-Pong. I won the intermediate championship at camp, the summer I was ten."

"Oh?"

"There was this old barn at Camp Ashcroft, called the Ping-Pong Palace. It had three Ping-Pong tables. I spent every minute I could in there; I lived and breathed Ping-Pong that summer. What a dumb thing to talk about, to a psychiatrist! What a waste of this appointment!"

"*This appointment,*" she echoes. Like someone repeating the punchline to a story, to make sure you get the point.

Okay, I got it: "*This appointment,* and *disappointment* sound alike." Maybe more alike to her; people not born here have trouble with *th*'s. Anyway, so what? I say superciliously, "Lots of words and phrases in the English language sound alike."

She says, "That is so," with a little smile at my tone, and tells me it's okay to talk about Ping-Pong all I want to, if that's what's on my mind.

"Well, I practiced, every chance I got. I developed a steady backhand, a low, fast serve. I beat everybody in the intermediate division, except one boy, Kevin Strauss, who had a tricky forehand slice. But then, on Parents' Weekend, I beat him, too. Just before I went in to play, I had this great moment of thinking, Hey,

44

some things I'm really good at! And I went ahead and won. Dad swung me up in the air. I remember looking down on the top of his head, his hair was all thick, didn't need styling. And Mom . . ." Wearing her moss-green wraparound skirt with the strawberry print . . . I loved that skirt, she'd had it since I was a baby. I remember, when I was little, trying to pick the strawberries off it. "Mom said she was proud of me. I sound like a ten-year-old, bragging."

"Let yourself," says Dr. Schneck.

"I got good at other camp activities. My parents brought up my flute, and I found the courage to play it on Talent Night. And swimming: I learned to relax in the water, swim distances without getting winded." Can't stop this bragging spree! "Then, next summer, I got into Mermaids, the most advanced swim group, and Isabella Fantano, the most popular counselor at Ash-croft, asked me to help choreograph the Mermaid Ballet, which made me an instant celebrity." I try to say this with the irony of looking back on childish things, but it comes out braggingly.

Some celebrity! Standing on a pile of smelly mattresses up in the damp, dark loft of the Ping-Pong Palace, on Saturday morning of Parents' Weekend, moistening my Camp Ashcroft T-shirt with spit, wiping years' worth of grime off the window, pressing my nose to the glass. . . .

The loft had no stairs or ladder. I'd stood on one of the tables and shimmied up a rafter, which gave me three splinters in my legs; luckily, big ones. I pulled them out easily.

The loft was used to store old junk, mattresses, stuff like that. I piled up three mattresses so I could reach the window way up high. I had to break a three-foot wide spiderweb to get near it. The spider had some bug victims wrapped up in spider spit to eat later on. I tried to set them free, but they were already dead.

I cleaned off the window with my shirt. This gave me a commanding view of the road that came spiraling up the base of Mount Ashcroft, and of all cars driving up to camp.

Parents were invited for noon. I was at my lookout post by ten thirty. My parents might be early. I had it all figured out in my head: They'd have started the trip on Friday. They'd have slept at a motel. After all, it was a long ride up from Rowayton to Ashcroft. I felt touched at the thought of the two of them cooped up together inside a car all those hours on my account. I wondered, would they have had separate rooms, or just separate beds, in the motel? And which car were they coming in?

First, hardly any cars came. To pass the time, I picked two numbers out of an imaginary hat: twenty-seven and nineteen. And I made bets: If I sighted the next car at the exact count of twenty-seven, it would be Dad's new silver Camaro. If at the count of nineteen, it would be Mom's tomato-red, still pretty new Datsun. I counted as regularly as a metronome, not cheating fate by slowing down or speeding up by so much as a beat. I counted to other numbers, sighted other cars. The system seemed to work. The numbers nineteen and twenty-seven seemed to hold themselves in reserve.

I was kind of rooting for the Datsun. I thought it was

the neatest car; I couldn't wait to be old enough to learn to drive it. Then, suddenly, out of the blue, I got this idea: Let their cars fight it out. Why not? It beat the method I'd been using, weighing all the pros and cons, changing my mind a hundred times a day, two hundred times at night. This would solve it, quick and simple: If the Camaro, Dad hit the jackpot; if the Datsun, Mom.

"You have been silent quite long," says Dr. Schneck.

"Sorry." Where was I? Oh, right, celebrity. "Another thing kids kind of envied me for, those with divorced parents—which was more than half the camp! They all had to live with their mothers whether they liked it or not. Whereas my parents were letting me choose. They thought that was pretty special." I check to see if Dr. Schneck's impressed.

"Of course, by now it's ancient history, and more parents are doing it that way. But I'm still proud of how they did it. I mean, divorce is so ordinary, almost more than staying married, at least they found a way to handle it differently, and be really fair about it. I think they deserve a lot of credit." I pause, to give her a chance to say she thinks so too.

"Well, anyway . . ." I tell how I watched from the loft of the Ping-Pong Palace, and about my scheme with the numbers 19 and 27. And my inspiration, letting the cars decide. "Of course," I quickly add, "that was just a game."

"Which car came?" asks Dr. Schneck.

"The Camaro—"

At ten minutes to twelve, so close behind a white VW I didn't have a chance to count. Sunlight exploded on

47

the windshield. Then it turned the curve, came into the shade, and I saw the empty passenger seat.

"With just Dad in it. Mom couldn't make it. There was a perfectly good explanation." Whew, I feel tired, all talked out, like anything else I'd say would take a great big effort. But I have to set her straight on this one thing: "Don't get the wrong idea: don't think I've been brooding over this all these years. I never even thought about it. Till just today. I don't know what made me bring it up."

She doesn't comment, just looks at me intently.

I feel dense all of a sudden, like a horse with blinders on. "Look, if *you* know something *I* don't know, I wish you'd tell me."

All she says is, "We will have a chance to talk more on Thursday."

This appointment's up.

IV

Thursday, April 14, 4:20–5:10 P.M.

It gives you a bigger jolt if you think of it yourself. How could I have missed it? It hit me like a fist in the face the second I walked out her door. Getting shrunk is weird: It goes on just as much, sometimes more, in corridors, elevators, and, right now, in this IRT (Intensely Repulsively Tormenting) subway train.

According to my watch, the time is 4:20. My session begins!

Opposite me sits a tough-looking blonde, bulging out of a puce-colored suit, holding a little kid in a scratchy-looking knitted outfit. He squirms. She jiggles him. He whines. She swats him. He shrieks.

49

"Tsk," goes the woman next to them, disapproving. She's in her fifties, looks beat. Next to her is an even older woman, Black, exhausted, looks as if she doesn't care what happens as long as she can stay sitting down.

Next to me, to my left, sits an ancient man. His clothes are much too big on him. He's so thin, he's almost transparent. Wiggly blue veins show through the skin of his head. He dozes, exhaling little gusts of breath that smells of garlic plus some kind of overripe fruit.

To my right sprawls a huge basketball-player type in a yellow T-shirt with *Cocaine* written on it in Coca-Cola script. His legs reach clear across the aisle. His skin-tight pants are metallic blue. His Adidas, largest size made, are yellow and blue, to match the outfit.

Graffiti artists have had a field day in this subway car. Everything's smeared up: windows, doors, advertising placards, subway maps, even the ceiling. What would archaeologists of the distant future (if there is one) make of these indecipherable scrawls?

My neighbor's fruit-and-garlic breath is starting to disagree with me. Or it's the salami, cheese, anchovies, olives, and other stuff I gobbled down to show how much I appreciated the trouble Gray went to.

Three minutes into my session! Can't this rotten joke of a train hurry up and creep faster?

Barnard has an old-fashioned requirement: two years of Phys. Ed. People gripe about it. It's okay with me, an excuse to spend time in the pool. I take Advanced Swimming Tuesdays and Thursdays. It lets out at 2:30. By the time I'd dressed and dried my hair, it was five of three.

I was going to walk to my session again, see what's blooming in the park, think in a leisurely way about things to talk about. But when I came out of Barnard Hall (the pool is in the basement), there was Gray. I thought for a second it was an optical illusion caused by underwater daydreaming while swimming all those laps. But optical illusions don't leap up from benches at you, or stick twigs of cherry blossoms in your pony-tail. Or carry two big bags from Murray's Delicatessen.

He wore his red cable-stitch sweater, hand-knit by his grandmother, and bright-orange Dawson Construction Company visor cap. He lit up the whole southeast section of the campus for me—would have, even in drab clothes.

"Hey, how come you're not in Vertebrate Embryology?"

"The weather's too great." (It still may be, for all I know, stuck down here in the bowels of the city.) "Wait till you taste all this stuff from Murray's. Here, raise your arms." He'd brought an extra sweater; it was windy out. He pulled it down over me. (I'm still wearing it, in this sweltering hell of a subway car.)

"I thought on a day like this we should have us a picnic, down at our meadow, what do you say?"

"Great!" As for my session, I figured if we hurried up, and if for once I splurged on a taxi, I could make it on time. I grabbed his hand, and we ran down to River-side Drive. We crossed through the park to the high-way, waited for a break in the traffic, and dashed across to a grassy place we'd discovered, amazingly free of beer cans and other trash, right at the edge of the Hudson.

A barge floated toward the George Washington Bridge. Big white gulls with yellow beaks circled in the air.

He'd even brought a tablecloth. And a bottle of Blanc de Blancs. "The man in the liquor store said it's as good as champagne—which this occasion calls for."

"Oh, really? What occasion is it?"

"Why," he said ceremoniously, "this here is the first annual Moskowitz-Dawson private outdoor pre-Passover, pre-Easter feast."

"Oh, Gray, that's beautiful!"

The Blanc de Blancs tasted more like vinegar, but we didn't care. It bubbled and fizzed just fine, and we drank a toast to our feast.

I started unwrapping the food.

"Wait, we'll eat later." He pulled me down in the grass.

"Not *too* much later," I said.

"Why? Is there someplace you'd rather be?"

"No. It's just that I have to leave at ten of four."

He leaned on the elbow and looked at me. His eyes had that silver-bright lit-from-the-inside look. "Why?" he traced the outline of my jaw. "Got another tooth-ache? Let's see if we can make it disappear. . . ."

One day last October I had raced down the 116th Street subway stairs, oblivious of everything but an awful toothache. Gray'd spotted me going into the station, went in too, got on the train. I didn't notice till he kissed the hand with which I was clutching my jaw.

Unlike the slow-motion trap I'm presently caught in, that train made good time. In less than ten minutes we

were down at Columbus Circle. Abracadabra, my tooth-
ache was gone! I called Dr. Frohman's office from the
nearest phone, said he wouldn't have to squeeze me in
between patients after all.

Arms around each other, Gray and I walked along
Central Park South. It was the first time we'd been in
that part of the city together. It's a wide, spectacular
street, full of out-of-towners. You can tell by the way
they carry their Bloomingdale's and Bergdorf Goodman
shopping bags, and from the slightly dazed looks on
their faces.

To our left the park spread out, nearly a thousand
acres of country in the middle of the city. Up ahead a
great architectural mix of older skyscraper towers with
delicate green-and-gilt tracings and new, unadorned,
geometrically shaped ones made of glass caught and
reflected the brilliant sun in the west. We felt as if
Manhattan had gotten itself up at its sumptuous, daz-
zling best, especially for us, for this unexpected bonus
afternoon together.

We'd synchronized our pace so that our thighs
touched with every step we took. When we got near
Fifth Avenue, we stood across from the Plaza Hotel,
craning our necks. We picked out three windows at the
top, inside a rounded tower, under a green slate dome.
We furnished ourselves a room up there, one as elaborate as Gray's room in his and Joe's apartment is plain.
We gave it every luxury: thick Oriental rugs; enormous
pillows; tall vases filled with chrysanthemums, asters,
zinnias, long-stemmed birds-of-paradise; crystal sconces
on the walls; a curved onyx and marble fireplace with

logs and kindling all prepared to be lit. We started the fire going. We tightened our arms around each other's waists; we were just about to dim the sconces when someone in a high silk hat and flowered vest standing beside a dappled horse called my name. He blended so well into the reverie, it took me a moment before I recognized him—Evan ("Heaven") Hendricks, with the knowing air and Mick Jagger swagger. Every girl in my high school class had hopes of going out with him. I had too, for the longest time.

"Dinah, great to see you!"

"Evan." Ditto. While he and I hugged, my two dates with him came back to me full blast, complete with let-down, once I knew he liked me. Meantime Gray stood beside the dappled horse, waiting, patting the horse's cheek. The whole time I hugged Evan, I kept my eyes locked into Gray's. We'd known each other five weeks, and it got better every day. Oh, please, let it keep on, I wished with all my might.

Evan had three jobs—tending bar, waiting tables, and this hansom cab job—trying to raise money for college next year. He insisted on driving Gray and me around in the park for fifteen minutes, his treat.

My only other ride like that was with Bobby Keller, after our senior prom. He was more of a good friend than a boyfriend of mine. We used to just have fun together. But on that formal evening, in the expensive moonlit setting, we'd felt called upon to act romantic and had ended up feeling like fools.

Whereas this ride with Gray—though we talked with Evan the whole time, and though it was broad daylight, and the weather still warm enough to waft the smell of horse dung to our noses—was the essence of romantic. Our eyes meeting often, our hands clasped together, were equal to the utmost contact. And my toothache was never heard from again. . . .

Two gray-and-white gulls flew down, spread out their feet on the water surface, swam off. I said, "Boy, I envy them."

"What for? Eating garbage soaked in Hudson River PCBs?"

"No, just that they're not about to have a heavy conversation." And I told Gray, "The reason I have to leave here at ten of four is, I'm going to a psychiatrist."

"Aw, come on." He was sure I was kidding. I had the amazing pain of watching his face go the whole distance from ready to laugh, to puzzled, to dismayed. "Why? What's bothering you? When did you start? How come you didn't tell me?"

It was as if I were turning into a different person, right before his eyes.

"Hey, there goes your cap!" A gust of wind snatched it up, blew it to the water. He didn't budge. I went after it; too late. It was already bobbing its way toward New Jersey.

"Forget it. It's just a dumb old cap. So, you're going to a psych-i-a-trist." He said it countrified and slow. He stuck a blade of grass between his teeth to heighten the effect of down-home boy, too simple to be told such things.

"Cut it out! Don't look so betrayed!"

"Sorry. I just had this notion you and I didn't keep secrets from each other. And that you were pretty happy."

"Say what you mean! You thought you were making me happy. Well, you are!"

Cathy Greenhaupt, my biology lab partner, is right; men are big egoists, always thinking whatever happens is their doing. Women are the same, though. I'd think the same thing if he sprang something like this on me. I tried to stroke his face. "I wish you wouldn't take it so personally."

He turned his face away. "What do you talk about to this psychiatrist guy?"

"It's a woman. Whatever comes into my mind. At least, that's the idea."

"And do you?"

"I know what you're thinking. Well, you're wrong! I don't tell intimate details about us."

"Yet," he said.

"No, Gray . . ." I started to promise, stopped in midsentence. If I made such a promise, I might as well stay at the picnic, forget the whole thing.

Gray said, "I guess you can't talk about it to me."

I said, "Come on, we have all this stuff; let's eat some." I tasted the cheese. "Mmm, great." I handed him some on a Triscuit with an olive. He put it down on the tablecloth.

I said, "Listen, next year, on the first anniversary of this feast, we'll bring cold fried Everglades frogs' legs, right? And instead of just gulls, we'll see herons, ibises, pelicans, maybe bald eagles—"

"Quit trying so hard."

So I shut up.

By then it was ten of four. But with things so not all right, I couldn't leave.

"You'll be late." Gray screwed the olive jar shut. "Don't worry about this stuff; I'll take it home." He packed it up. I helped. He started to fold the tablecloth.

I grabbed two corners. We joined the edges together. Just at the moment our fingers met—as if our touching could generate such power—a bunch of gulls flapped into the air with one big rush of wings.

I put my hands on Gray's shoulders. He didn't back away. He put his hands on my shoulders. "Sorry I took it like that. I guess I'll get used to the idea." Then he said such a sweet thing, so far off the mark! That as far as he was concerned, I'm perfect, so the only thing wrong he could think of had to be him. "Dinah, I just love you such a lot. Hey, girl, that's no reason to cry." He kissed the tears off my face. One thing led to another. It was a minute to four when we left that place.

Damn! In the middle of crossing Riverside Drive, I suddenly remembered, that morning, on the bus to school, I'd paid Julie back five dollars I owed her. I checked my wallet. All I had was $3.92. Not enough for a taxi. And Gray only had thirty-eight cents after buying all that stuff.

"I'll take the subway down to Seventy-second and get a taxi crosstown; I have enough for that. Bye, talk to you later." I ran up the block to the station.

While I was buying a token, a train pulled in. I

hurled myself through the turnstile and took the stairs down to the platform so fast, I nearly sprawled on the floor. When I reached the doors, they'd shut three quarters of the way, impossible to squeeze in.

I waited on the platform eleven minutes. Finally this mockery of a train pulled in and crawled incredibly slowly and maddeningly close to Seventy-second Street— only to grind to a dead halt in the totally dark tunnel. Then the inside lights went out. The last look I had at my watch was at 4:34—fourteen minutes into my session!

Across the aisle the little kid is screaming. The huge guy to my right starts to move his thigh on top of mine. I stand up. Where's a strap? I find one and hang on, in case we ever lurch to a start.

Thank you, David L. Gunn, head of the MTA, Metropolitan Transit Authority. (*Transit* is a broken promise; we're not going anywhere!) Thanks a lot, all of you eminent people on that Authority, and Mayor Koch, and Governor Cuomo, and who all else's fault the New York City subway system is. If I had a spray can, I'd spray on some graffiti of my own, only the words would be legible.

4:38: Lights come on. Train lurches forward, makes it into the station.

4:40: Three steps at a time, up into daylight, onto the island in the intersection of Broadway and Seventy-second Street. A taxi comes. I grab it.

4:55: I shove the $3.02 left after buying a token at the driver, rush past the dignified uniformed doorman into the building, press the Up button, wait another eternal minute for the elevator to descend.

4:56½: Finger on the buzzer, insides in an uproar. Did she get fed up waiting for me, go out shopping or for a walk? Or, if she's in there, will she try to sell me (I've heard psychiatrists do this) the idea that somewhere deep down inside me, I *wanted* to come late?

She buzzes me in.

"I was stuck in the subway! You won't believe me! The train just stopped dead, for nearly half an hour!"

She says, "I also sometimes take the subway. I believe you," and sits back to listen.

Out pours the whole story of our stormy picnic, my subway imprisonment, no *um*'s or pauses. "Of all times for this to happen! When I had something I couldn't wait to tell you! And when we were going to decide if I should continue. . . ." In the middle of this I become aware, I already *have* decided.

"We still can," she says.

"I want to continue. Till I leave for London."

"Fine."

So now I tell her what hit me, leaving here last time: "Remember, *this appointment* and *disappointment*? You were right. They were connected. And not just by the sound of the words."

"How else?"

"Well, it started with your disappointing me. Not buzzing back. If that hadn't happened, I probably wouldn't even have thought of Parents' Weekend, Mom not showing up. Only calling that a disappointment was the understatement of the year."

"What would you call it?"

"It felt more like the end of the world. When I saw Dad in the car alone, I thought Mom was . . ." No use, I can't bring it past my lips. I try the other way around. "When you didn't answer the buzzer, I thought you . . ." No use this way either. Sticks and stones, that old saying, may be true, but my tongue's on strike, won't form the words.

"You thought something had happened to me. You thought I was dead," says Dr. Schneck with a cheeriness I'd like to hug her for.

"Right. And Mom . . . Well, I just refused to imagine anything less catastrophic. And I did a crazy thing: chased straight up the mountain, took the steepest path, covered with poison ivy. I got parched. I climbed till I was past exhaustion, past caring about anything, or anybody. . . ."

"But when you started out," Dr. Schneck starts quietly, "you cared a tremendous amount, wouldn't you say? You felt—"

"*Angry,* you were going to say, weren't you? Well, you're wrong, I wasn't!"

Her gaze is full of sympathy. Her hands move to the arms of her chair. "We must stop here for today. I will see you Monday."

"Okay." How do other patients manage? Stuff their despairs with jagged edges into an invisible drawstring bag, pull the strings, tie a knot, keep it shut till next time, wish her happy holidays, and go enjoy themselves, act normal at their seders and/or happy Easters?

V

Monday, April 18, 3:40–4:30 P.M.

"How were your holidays?"

"Wild. Not the holidays, *I* was. Dad's not talking to me. I'm on the outs with Mom too. Oh, and I have orders to 'Take up my hostility toward Audrey' with you. Okay, I'll do that right away: Audrey is as silly and synthetic as the products it's her chosen career to push the American public into throwing away money on. Audrey Gerstein gives me one large pain. You should have seen her at the seder...."

Dr. Schneck looks pretty. No snail-color scheme today. Her blouse, of some delicate material, voile or chiffon, is the color of burgundy. It reminds me of the

61

stained-glass lamp over my grandparents' dining-room table when they lived in Brooklyn. (They live in Florida now. "I can visit them when I'm down there," I've told Dad, to reconcile him to my plans. He just answers, "You could, anyway.") "When I was little, we always went to my grandparents' house for Passover. I'd rather tell you about a seder back then, okay?"

She does her open-hands gesture.

"I was eight. When Mom wasn't looking, Grandma Ida poured real Manischewitz, not grape juice, in my glass. Grandpa Morris said a blessing. Everybody sipped. I loved the wine! Nothing so red and rich had ever passed my lips before. I loved how it burned, going down my throat. My insides felt aglow. Grandpa Morris said more blessings. I took more sips. Pretty soon the room was turning. I felt as if the me that was sitting at the table was just my outer shell, and the real me was floating up toward the lamp. Poor uncles, aunts, etc., sitting on their chairs like lumps! I thought, Thank you, God, for wafting me up and letting me glide gloriously around. I'd gotten so drunk, I fell deeply asleep right after the gefilte fish and matzoh-ball soup, which always were the best parts of the meal, anyhow. Next thing I knew, I was home, in my bed. Mom and Dad lifted me out of the car and carried me upstairs without waking me up. I can't imagine what this is relevant to."

"Don't worry."

"Okay, back to the seder at my Aunt Ro and Uncle Sidney's, last Thursday. Naturally Audrey came. Flashing her new pearl-and-ruby bracelet, from Guess Who,

for everyone to gush over. She held it to the candle-
light. She nearly blinded Uncle Sidney. As it was he had
trouble reading from the Haggadah. He's not the He-
brew scholar my Grandpa Morris is.

"My cousin Jonathan, age nine, asked the questions.

"After dinner I went and kept him company while he
got ready for bed. I said, 'You should have asked a fifth
question: Wherefore, on this night, doesn't God smite
Audrey off her chair?'

"Just that moment Dad came in. 'Very nice, Dinah.
So respectful and mature of you! Why don't you take
up your hostility to Audrey with Dr. Schneck?'

" 'Who's Dr. Schneck?' Jonathan asked.

"I was furious with Dad for bringing you up. I didn't
want to show it and give him the satisfaction. So I made
up this whole elaborate pretend game about you—I
hope you don't mind. I said, 'Well, you see, Jonathan,
Dr. Schneck's a snail doctor.' I got down on all fours,
scrunched my head into my shoulders, stuck my fingers
out like snail antennae, crept around the room. . . ."
Acting like a nine-year-old! I ask myself, How does this
jibe with the grown-up-woman me, last night, on the
blanket, at the stables? . . .

"Go on," says Dr. Schneck.

"Jonathan loved it. He asked, 'Who'd go to a snail
doctor? Other snails?'

" 'Exactly. Grasshoppers, katydids, ladybugs, worms,
little animals like that.' I wiggled my finger-antennae
at him. He climbed on my back. I gave him a ride.
'What's hostility?' he asked.

" 'When you want to knock somebody down.' I

bounced him off. 'Pow, pow.' I make-believe punched him.

"Dad was getting exasperated. 'Jonathan, I came in here to say good night to you.'

" 'Good night, Uncle Nick. Giddyap, snail, or I'll punch you, pow!' Dad went out, banged the door. One thing he can't stand is when people ignore him.

"Yesterday, at Mom's, well, it started out fine, ended up bad. With me breaking this little cream pitcher from Grandma Otis. It's part of a set of dessert dishes I'm supposed to have when I get married. Of course it was an accident. I felt awful about it. . . ." And other things, too. "I needed to get out of there. I made Gray leave, even though he was having a good time."

Then came the magic part of the night. . . .

"You know that ceramic over the couch in your waiting room?" An oval-shaped, beautiful madonna and child. Like by Della Robbia. The child is reaching up; he looks so alive and full of mischief, you think he's about to grab a curl of the madonna's hair. And she's so young, she looks so blissful, as if the greatest fun and happiness in the world is playing with a pudgy baby on your lap.

I fold my arms over my breasts. My nipples are sticking out. Just from thinking about last night, after we left Mom's. Oh, I take all of this very seriously; that I'm sitting in this chair, that I have the opportunity to talk about my problems. I don't pretend anymore that I don't have any. It's just that last night, in the moonlight, on the blanket on the ground, was *not* a problem; in fact, the opposite!

64

What should I talk about instead? I know: resume where I left off last time: Dad coming up to camp alone. I tell how I threw myself on the pile of mattresses up in the Ping-Pong Palace loft, straw ends sticking up out of the ticking, scratching my face. And I cried, I howled, really loud, though no one could hear me. "Mom, oh, Mom!"

"You have to realize," I explain to Dr. Schneck, "my mother never missed a single occasion when her presence was officially required, not even after she went back to finish college. She came to all parent-teacher conferences, school plays, music school recitals during my flute years, dance recitals during my dance years, riding meets during my horse years. Well, Parents' Weekend was a thousand times more important! *Everybody's* parents came. The ones who were out of the country made it their business to be back in time. Getting divorced was no excuse, either.

"You see, Mom was on this dig in Arizona. She'd written me that she'd be flying to New York on Thursday, would spend the night at home, and would drive up to camp with Dad. Well, the plane might have crashed. . . . Or it could have happened in the car. . . . Mom, all tan, her hair sun-bleached, on her way, where to? To the drugstore, to buy me the herbal shampoo I'd asked for? To the Book Nook, because I was fresh out of books?

"I pictured the Datsun backing onto the road. The road gets overgrown in summer, branches hanging low, blocking the view. And another car careening down the hill. I all but heard the clash and crunch of metal. I squeezed my eyes shut. Still, I saw the Datsun folded up, totaled, fastened to Don's Texaco Tow Truck, being towed on its last trip—what a thing to think of! *Cars* are replaceable."

It's very still in here. These windows must be made of extra thick glass. Traffic noises sound faraway. An ambulance siren starts up, but it's only the faintest wail.

"From the other window in the Ping-Pong Palace loft I could see out over the flagpole field, where parents and kids were having reunions, laughing and kissing. I could see Dad alone, looking around; where was I? Wondering—used to working from a script—how was he going to tell me?

"Ready, set, I jumped down any old way, so what if I broke anything, it couldn't hurt more than I already hurt.

"I stole around to the far side of the building, hugging the wall, so no one would see me. I crossed an unmowed field. The tall grass hid me. I made for the woods, took the steep trail up Mount Ashcroft.

"I had slippery sandals on, no socks, and just shorts and a sleeveless T-shirt. I was a moving feast for mosquitoes. Thorns and thistles scratched me too; so what? And I stepped right in the poison ivy.

"It was a hot day. I climbed fast. There no brooks or waterfalls. Fine. I figured, the rougher it got, physically, the less I'd feel my despair. It worked. I climbed for I don't know how long. Till I dropped from thirst and exhaustion. I didn't care if I ever got up again.

66

"Meantime the whole camp, except for the tadpole division, was out looking for me.

"Dr. Pinkhuys, the camp director himself, led the search party that found me. He was a lean, tall man, with white hair and a white beard. He held a branch that he'd used for a walking staff. He looked like a little kid's idea of God, acted it too, lectured the whole camp on Sundays about having 'moral fiber,' being 'staunch,' and 'above all, considerate of others.'

"He checked me over to make sure I had a pulse and nothing obvious was out of whack. Then he let me have it. Never in his forty years at Ashcroft had anyone done so despicable a deed. He'd had to ask the police to join in the search. They thought I might have drowned; they were going to dredge the lake. How had I dared to cause all this trouble? Not to mention cause my father so much anguish and fear? Could I think of any reason why he, Dr. Pinkhuys, should not send me home in disgrace?

"No, all I would think of was, Mom was okay. Or he'd have acted sorry for me.

"When I got back, all my bunkmates were out searching. Only Dad was in there, sitting on my bed, hunched over, head in his hands. 'Hey, Dad . . .'

"He just held me. Didn't ask questions. Didn't blame me. After a while he said he should have let me know ahead of time. He'd thought it would be easier if he told me when he saw me.

"Mom had decided to fly to New York a day later, come straight up to camp from Kennedy. And she'd missed her plane, that was all. Couldn't get on another flight. 'Wait. She'll call. She'll explain it to you herself.'

"She did. During Parents' Night dinner. The loud-speaker came on. Mrs. Herbert, the camp secretary, paged me, 'phone call for Dinah Moskowitz.'

"Dad went with me to the camp office building.

"At the sound of Mom's voice, I got that parched feeling that I'd had up on the mountain, not just in my mouth and throat. All through me. I squeezed the phone to my ear, like my ear could lap it up. She sounded really close, more like in the next building than three quarters of America away.

"She was calling from Gallinas Springs, halfway between the dig site and the Albuquerque airport. It was such a tiny place; all it had was a gas station, store, and saloon, like an old John Wayne movie set. There wasn't even a motel. The couple who owned the gas station had kindly let her spend the night in their spare room.

"The pickup truck she was driving had sprung a leak in its radiator. The garage in Gallinas Springs couldn't fix it; they had to send for a new one to another town, which was pretty far away. They got one finally and put it in. Now here was the situation: She could take a plane out of Albuquerque tomorrow, Sunday, not a direct flight. She'd have to change in Atlanta, Georgia. But she could be at Kennedy by Sunday night, and up at camp first thing Monday morning. Dr. Pink-huys discouraged parents from visiting any other time except Parents' Weekend. But she didn't care. 'Di-zey, do you?'

"She hadn't called me by that name in ages. She asked, 'Do you want me to come?'

I tell this quite matter-of-factly. " 'How's the dig going, Mom?' I'm still proud how I asked that. And then I said, 'No, Mom. It's okay. You don't have to come.'

"Dad squeezed my hand.

"Mom asked, 'Are you sure?' A crackling came into the wires. I couldn't hear her that well. She said she'd be looking for good presents for me and, 'See you on the sixteenth.'

"Walking back from the camp office building to the dining hall, I noticed that fog was rolling in, wrapping up the top part of Mount Ashcroft like in a thick blanket. Good. I'd keep the part of me that had rushed up there under wraps too.

"Everything worked out okay. Dr. Pinkhuys let me stay. The other Mermaids and Isabella Fantano forgave me. The Mermaid Ballet was rescheduled for Sunday. I swam and dived my heart out. It was a big success. The rest of the summer went fine.

"After it, though, I never wanted to see Camp Ashcroft again. I started going to Silverbirch as a camper for three summers, then a C.I.T., then regular counselor, and this summer, I already told you. I'm really looking forward to it." My voice kind of gives out. I've been talking so much, my throat's dry.

She asks me what I'm thinking.

"Wondering if I should go get a drink of water." There are Dixie cups in the bathroom. No, too embarrassing to walk out, come back in. "The other thing I'm thinking of is this party my parents gave, when I was little. I guess being thirsty reminded me. . . ."

69

I was seven. I'd pestered them to stay up late. I passed around—and ate—anchovies, salty peanuts, stuff like that.

I woke up in the middle of the night or early morning with my mouth as dry as now.

The house was quiet.

I went down the backstairs to the kitchen. My bunny pajamas had soft padded feet; I didn't make a sound. I thought I'd get some ginger ale or soda. But Mom and Professor Levinson stood blocking the refrigerator door. He was head of the archaeology department at Sarah Lawrence, the college Mom was going to. The reason I thought it was Dad was, I thought only married people ever pressed up against each other that close, almost occupying the same space. Their four shoes stood in a row, Mom's high-heeled silver evening sandals between his huge, long, shiny black loafers on the white vinyl floor. I'd flicked the light switch on. For a second Mom opened her eyes. She saw me; she must have. She shut her eyes again, quick. Shut me out.

I tell this to Dr. Schneck. It's a molehill memory, not to be made a big mountain of. It's just something that happened, that's all.

At the end of the session I'm annoyed at myself that I didn't get to Easter Sunday—I mean, the part before the crystal cream pitcher broke. I feel as though I've jumped around from one thing to another and nothing got connected to anything. "This isn't doing much good," I say as I leave. Yet I'm impatient for Thursday, wish it were tomorrow.

VI

Thursday, April 21, 4:20–5:10 P.M.

"Outside this room spring's galloping past. The for-
sythia and daffodils are already over. In here time
moves so slow! Or else it's me, *I'm* slow. Like last time,
I couldn't even get through what happened in *one*
weekend! I know what you're going to do now, make
that motion with your hands, put them palms up in
your lap. That's your way of saying, there's lots of time.
Well, there isn't, not for me! I can't back out of the
trip; Dad would be too hurt. It's less than a month
away. And I won't have gotten anywhere!"

Up go her glasses, into her hair, so there's nothing

between her green gaze and me. "Where is it you want to get?"

"I don't know." I gaze away. "Out of the holes I fall into. To where I can stop feeling that I'm failing at a whole bunch of things, that I'm not worth this attention." If I go on, I'll fall into a deep hole right now. The hell with it! "Why is it always so hard to get started?"

Hey, she raised the blinds behind the plants. Good for you, begonias, ferns, etc., get your daylight and sun!

I half close my eyes. I gaze at the ferns through the curtain of my lashes, metamorphose them into great palms surrounding our Everglades cabin, Quonset hut, shack, whatever. The palm fronds shade the hammock in which I laze, pudgy baby at my breast. The baby's naked. No, got a diaper on. Make that a Whooshy. Because regardless of how angry and disillusioned Dad would be, he'd still send us down a big supply of those. The baby finds my nipple, sucks. I close my eyes all the way, try to imagine the sensation of milk flowing out of my breasts.

Dr. Schneck says, "You seem faraway in your thoughts. Would you like to tell me about them?"

No. Not my Everglades idyll. I press the side of my head.

"Do you have a headache?"

"Kind of. I've had one, off and on, all day." It started in Mrs. Donadio's office. She called me in this morning and gave me a hard time. I tell about that.

"Dinah, you've let me down." She went to Hunter High herself. Maybe she's extra hard on Hunter graduates. In any case, she was on the warpath. "With all your enthusiasm (she was one of my interviewers when I applied) for poetry, philosophy, journalism, languages, you didn't seem like the kind of student who'd be doing C work in two subjects. Why?"

"Oh, I guess anthropology was a mistake. I took it only to please Mom. And I'm just no good at dissecting worms. I get butterfingers as soon as I walk into bio lab. I'm going into debt from breaking all those slides."

She wears her glasses on a beaded chain, hanging down. She bounced them impatiently against her big shelf of a bosom; she'd heard those excuses too often. The reason she'd called me in was I'd missed the deadline for filing a fall program.

"But Mrs. Donadio, I've been planning to tell you, I won't be in school next fall. I'm going to—"

"Spare me. You can go to Mars, to the moon, but you'll still make out a program. That's the rule. It can be tentative." She dumped the fall catalog in my lap. "Go ahead; right now."

I opened it to four random pages, the *I Ching* method, wrote down the first four courses that met my eye: The Politics of Policy Making in Defense and Foreign Affairs. American Music. Complex Variables. And, no kidding, Hormones and Reproductive Behavior.

"Not *that* tentative!" She ripped up the form. "Now, you listen": She grew up poor, worked her way through college being a stock clerk at Ohrbach's, she has no patience with people who get their education handed to them on a silver platter and want to toss it out the window. "Here." She handed me another form. "Make it out. More believably."

I did.

"Okay, now, get out of here." She gave me a caustic smile, and a whack, not that light, on the behind with her eyeglass case. So it is not my head that should be hurting.

"My friend Julie Warshkower gets headaches. Her shrink, Terry, says they're psychosomatic. This Terry is on a campaign to make her more able to accept 'mothering.' It hasn't started to work yet. Julie and her mom still slam doors in each others' faces, have such noisy fights, the neighbors complain. Not like Mom and me. We're real quiet. We just make each other nervous. I get a head start; I get nervous before I even go there."

Dr. Schneck asks, "Why is that?"

"I guess because I admire her so much. She has her whole life in control, does everything perfectly with a minimum of fuss, so it all looks easy—teaches, writes articles, runs the house, puts on great meals, does the garden, you name it.

"Anyway, on Sunday I started out more confident than usual. I'd put my outfit together carefully: smart new khaki skirt, oatmeal linen jacket; I thought I looked my best. I liked the idea of going there with Gray. Mom thinks a lot of him.

"Dad was still miffed about 'my attitude to Audrey,' but he let us have the car, which was nice of him. It's a Volvo. It handles really well. Since I was picking up Gray, I went up the West Side, took the Merritt Parkway. It's less direct than the Thruway, but it's truck-and billboard-free and the scenery is pretty.

"The ride up was great. The farther north we went, the less advanced the leaves on bushes and trees were. Gray said it was like getting back the part of spring we'd already used up.

"I steered with my left hand. With my right, I picked up his hand, put it to my lips . . ." like a little taste, in advance. "We turned on the radio. You know how sometimes the thing you're most in the mood to listen to comes on? Well, WQXR was playing *The Creation,* by Haydn. We're just reading Book VII of *Paradise Lost* in my Milton course. Most of the text is from there, so I knew what was coming. 'Gray, listen, this next part's for you!' I said.

" 'And God created great whales,' the Archangel Raphael sang, and we sang along, at the top of our lungs, 'and every living creature that moveth; and God blessed them, saying—' "

I stop right there. I don't tell what God said: "Be fruitful all, and multiply." I keep that to myself.

"When we left the parkway, we lost the station. Approaching, um . . ." I stumble over the word *home,* change it to *Rowayton.* What I meant was, the nearer we came, the more nervous I got.

"This is Gray's fourth northeastern spring. He's still not used to it. He couldn't get over how fantastic the place looked. Daffodils, hyacinths, scilla, every kind of tulip out in splendor. It would have made a great color-spread in *House & Garden* or some magazine like that."

75

"You sound sad," says Dr. Schneck.

"Well, I used to do things in the garden—weed, plant bulbs. Dad did too. We both had pretty green thumbs. You'd never guess. The place looks just as good without us. Anyhow, Gray was impressed. With Mom, too, in her blue jeans and sweater, with her light hair blowing around her face. *His* mother—I've seen photos—was once very pretty, but is overweight now and wears her hair beauty-parlor neat and ladylike.

"We had the usual awkward moment of wondering who'll hug whom first and being glad when that's out of the way.

"Gray complimented her on the garden. She complimented me on my outfit. I felt overdressed, as though every minute of my putting it together showed.

"Mom's tenants, the Androwskys, were there. Nadia is studying architecture. They're both really handy. They turned our former family room into a living space for themselves. Mom let them break through to the garage so they could put in a neat little kitchen and bathroom.

"And Ellen Steinfeld, my childhood best friend. The Steinfelds lived across the brook from us. Now they live in Hartford. Ellen goes to Wesleyan, takes a course with Mom.

"Also, there was this archaeologist from North Dakota, Professor McVeigh. I don't know if Mom invited him just to be hospitable, or if she's interested in him. Anyway, he seemed nice.

"Dinner was delicious. Everybody seemed relaxed. The conversation flowed. Everybody had a great time. . . ."

76

"Except you?" asks Dr. Schneck.

"Right. I went into a quiet tailspin. I felt out of it. Everybody else seemed to belong there more than me. I couldn't think of a thing to contribute. Finally—I couldn't sit there like a dummy anymore—I made this blooper." The blood rushes to my face, just thinking about it. "It was so stupid, I don't want to say it."

"Say it anyway."

"Well, Tom Androwsky, who's an amateur ornithologist, had just finished saying that ospreys were making a good comeback; he'd spotted an occupied nest down near the beach. I said, yes, and wasn't it terrific, how, back in the seventies, they rescued the snailstarter? Remember, sometime back then, this tiny little fish was going to die out unless they stopped constructing a dam in Tennessee, and the Supreme Court ruled they had to, so that was great, only, I got the name wrong. Everybody kindly refrained from laughing. It's called the snail*d*arter.

"I was embarrassed to death. I got busy clearing the table, but was actually fleeing. Ellen and Nadia Androwsky started to clear too, but Mom asked them to stay seated; she preferred it that way.

"Finally she and I had a moment alone together in the kitchen. It was the first moment all day. She came over to me, close, let the tip of her nose touch the tip of mine. We did that when I was little. She was embarrassed too, but she laughed and told me not to feel so bad; everybody sometimes gets things wrong.

"I said, 'Mom, you know what? I've been thinking of telling you. . . .' "

The way Dr. Schneck looks at me, I think she knows what it was. I ask her, "Do you know what I was going to tell Mom?"

She gives me her friendliest look, head-on.

"Well, *do* you?"

She asks, "Is this a test?"

"What if it is?" And I think, You're flunking it!

"Why do you need to test me?"

I shrug. "Why won't you answer my question?"

It's a stand-off.

"Well, anyway, I couldn't tell Mom anything, because just then the phone rang. Mom answered, 'Hello?'

"She and I sound alike on the phone. I stood next to her, so I could hear Joe say, 'Hey, Dynamite.'

" 'No, this is Dinah's mother.' Mom got this funny look on her face. I could almost hear her thinking, Dinah might what? What's my daughter up to? . . . She handed me the phone.

Joe said he had to go over to Lucky's, Lucky needed him for something. Did I know where the box of dried flies for Bartram could be? He'd looked everywhere. Bartram is Gray's pet sandsnake.

"I said, 'On the shelf under his cage, maybe behind some books.'

"Joe said, 'Thanks. Hope I didn't interrupt your dinner.'

" 'No, that's okay. Say hello to Lucky for me.' I hung up.

"Mom was getting ready to take out dessert. She put a cake on a platter. She asked me to take the cream out of the refrigerator. She filled the matching crystal sugar bowl up with sugar. She wasn't looking at me, but I could see, she still had that expression on her face. She asked me, 'Just how serious are you about Gray?'

"It really bothered me. I thought of Grandma Otis. She died when I was six; I only saw her a couple of times in my life. She was a proper midwestern lady with blue-tinted hair. When I was born, she crocheted me a pink sweater and baby hat. *She* never had a chance to ask Mom such a question. She didn't meet my father till after Mom and he were married. . . . I thought of Professor Levinson. How serious was Mom about *him*, that night when they'd stood right there, kissing? 'Pretty serious, Mom,' I answered in a calm, steady voice, and down went the pitcher, crash. A big lake of cream spread over the tiles, with little jagged islands of crystal sticking up.

"Mom's face said, You've smashed everything dear to me in the whole world. Mom *said*, 'Never mind, these things happen.' We knelt down and picked up the pieces—of the cream pitcher. Not of being together."

I stretch my legs out, let my shoulders slump, let a gust of breath out. I straighten up and ask, "*Do* you know what I was on the verge of telling Mom before the phone rang?"

She still won't answer.

"In your psychiatric training, did you have a course on how to look inscrutable in perpetuity?"

I like how unruffled she stays. She says, "I do understand your wanting to test me. You want to see if I'm in tune with your thoughts and feelings. But it really would be much more helpful if you would try and express these things in words."

"Okay, sure, I want you to be 'in tune.' I *know* you know what I was going to tell Mom." I tell it to Dr. Schneck: "About 'snailstarting.' I laugh. "About coming to you."

She smiles. "It's an interesting slip of the tongue."

Slip of the tongue; hey, I like it. It's more elegant than blooper. Session's over. I feel good. Maybe a snailstarter's not such a bad thing to be.

VII

Monday, April 25, 3:40–4:30 P.M.

"Something's wrong with Joe's Uncle Lucky. He's a really robust man; you'd never think of him as sick or needing anything. Well, on Easter Sunday, for the second time that week, he fell down the steps outside his apartment building. That's why Joe had to go there. Joe's worried. Lucky hates doctors. If it happens again, Joe'll have to drag him to go see one. I don't know why I'm telling you this. It doesn't have to do with me. Except, well, I feel very close to Joe as a friend."

Change of topics: "By the way, I've changed my mind about something."

"Yes?"

"Remember when you said people in therapy start to listen to themselves? I thought, Wow, big deal; what can they find out that way? Well, I found some things out, listening to my 'slip of the tongue.' "

"What things?"

I like it when she gets that eager look of wanting to hear. "*I'm* the snailstarter. Every session, it's so hard to get started. Then, when I do, I don't cover much ground. Um, I'm slow at other things, too."

Covering ground, literally, outside the stable. A shiver goes over me. My body remembers how it was—finally!

"Go on," says Dr. Schneck.

No Trespassing, the sign said. . . . "I had snails on the brain the whole weekend," I say in a joking voice. "Already at the seder. Kidding around with Jonathan. And that night, I dreamed . . ."

She sits forward. Dreams are shrinks' cups of tea.

"All I remember is one little glimmer: You came to the seder. As if you belonged, as if you always came to our family seders. I was glad. That's it.

"The main thing I found out from my 'snailstarter' slip—this'll be hard to explain: all the time I got ready to go to Mom's, all during the drive up there, I was already planning to tell her about coming to you. I was looking forward to it. Only, I didn't know it. That sounds really strange, but do you know what I mean?"

She nods.

"There's a poem by Keats in which the explorer Cortez stands on a mountain peak and a whole new ocean, the Pacific, stretches out below. All I did was make one bl—I mean, slip of the tongue, so it's a fancy comparison, I know: *I* feel like an explorer. Here. Of the hidden parts of me. In which I've been busy thinking things, doing things, all these years, not on the sly, exactly. Just with a *No Trespassing* sign up to the rest of me. It's scary; it's exciting. Not to psychiatrists, I suppose. Psychiatrists know all about it, don't you? You have technical words for it: Subconscious? Unconscious? Which is it? You hear about it all the time; it must be old hat to you."

"The day it starts to be 'old hat' to me, I will stop seeing patients. 'The hidden parts of you' says it fine; I prefer it to technical language."

I feel pleased. "Good, I'm glad." What happens next is a big surprise: Out comes the part of Easter Sunday I'd determined *not* to tell. And for some of it I even look her in the face:

"Right after dessert I said, 'Dad wants the car back by eleven,' which wasn't true. And Gray and I left Mom's.

"I got in the car on the driver's side. He said, 'I thought you didn't like to drive at night.'

" 'Tonight I feel like it.' *Vroom*, gravel spurted up from the driveway and clattered against the sides of the car.

"One thing I was thankful for: He didn't bug me with questions like, What's the rush, what did I drag him away for? He just sat there quietly, practicing northeastern tree identification, not that easy to do when all you have to go by is their silhouettes in the dark. 'Maple, dogwood, wild cherry, hawthorn.' And he didn't go into a rhapsody on how terrific Mom is, as my friends tend to do after I've taken them there. Not that I wouldn't have agreed. I just was in no mood for it then.

"The traffic light right before the Thruway was red. While we were stopped at it, he did ask, 'What broke when you were out in the kitchen?'

" 'Let's not talk about it, okay?'

" 'Okay.' He leaned over, gave me a quick kiss.

"I know that light; it's a long one. I pulled him back over, kissed him at length.

"Cars behind us started honking. The light had changed. Okay, I stepped on the gas.

"Gray said, 'I guess you didn't have the greatest Easter.'

"I said, 'True, but it isn't over yet.'

" 'Hey, didn't you just pass the entrance to the Thruway?' "

"Right. It was a slip of the foot. 'Guess what?' I said. 'I'm abducting you.'

"He went, 'Mmm, sounds good,' leaned his head against the headrest, closed his eyes. I could see his Adam's apple moving in his throat. 'Abduct away.'

"I drove through Darien, out toward New Canaan. I remembered the way perfectly: Left on Stanhope, up Birch Hill to where the road forks; left again, up a rutted dirt road—luckily the Volvo has good springs— to Wide Skies Stables.

"I parked at the near end of the barn. 'This is where I used to ride. Want to see the place?'

" 'Sure. What about this sign, though? It says *No Trespassing*.'

" 'It's okay; nobody'll see us. If they do, I'll just say

84

I'm showing you around. They'll remember me. Come on.'

"I showed him the paddock where I had my first lesson, on Thunderbolt, an average-size horse, but he'd seemed gigantic to me, his neck stretching out like a mountain slope before me. I was terrified, hung on for dear life. But I was also thrilled to be so high off the ground, my head reaching into the sky.

"I showed him the other paddock, where the horse shows and meets used to be. And the place on the path leading out of the barn where my favorite horse, Cherokee—I used to bring him apples!—chucked me in the mud one time.

"The moon rose. The wind died down. I said, 'Wait here a second, okay?'

"I went to the car, got an old blanket out of the trunk. I spread it on the ground in the wind-sheltered corner where the barn and stable join.

"Gray put his arms around me. 'Is it okay for the abductee to hold the abductor?'

" 'Absolutely.' I stood on my toes. There's so many different kinds of kisses, a whole language of them. The way we kissed just then was like . . . I can't say it."

"Try."

"Like trumpets proclaiming . . . I have to go back and explain. I haven't told you how it's been. Um, not that great. We weren't—I wasn't—doing that well before." I leave out some details. I can't face her right at the moment. But I manage to sum up what the state of our "practicing" was.

"Well, finally, Easter Sunday night, it started to be

more like what I used to imagine. Being outdoors, even the cold, even that my carefully put-together outfit got rumpled and squeezed, only added to it.

"I kept my eyes open. Usually I have them shut tight. But there was so much to see: new grass shooting up around us. Moonlit fences. Clumps of birches. Woods beyond. Puffs of clouds, moon and stars overhead. And all the fantastic night colors, milky blues, bluish whites, mauve, maroon, purple, and incredibly beautiful midnight blue.

"I usually get really bothered if I can't shut out my thoughts. Well, it didn't worry me. I just let whatever thoughts came along wander freely through: Like, how technology can make the most complicated products— synthetics, plastics, lasers, microchips—but nothing that feels even remotely like skin. And if fingertips could sing, mine would have, whole long songs in praise of skin, all the more finger-beguiling when you come to it finally, after digging through layers of clothes.

"Gray had his eyes open too. For once that corny phrase came true, seeing stars in somebody's eyes.

"Then we changed positions and the stars went back up into the sky, where they're supposed to be.

"Then I heard this noise, a rippling, cascading sound, wild. It sounded like inside my head, expressing what was happening in me. But it was a horse, neighing in the barn behind us—my spokeshorse, I said later. Gray knew what I meant.

"Then there was this huge silence, into which Gray said *Dinah*. And the whole silence filled up with my name as if nobody had ever uttered it before. As if he'd just invented it, and along with it, my whole new self that could experience such sensations.

"I wanted it to last forever. But he raised himself up, almost out of me, and he asked, 'Is it safe?'

"I pulled him down by the shoulders and gripped him to me with all the strength in my arms and my thighs. I twisted my legs around his and crossed my ankles so he wouldn't break loose and pull out of me in case he suddenly remembered that I'd gotten my period exactly two weeks before." I tell this part of the story to the Levolors. "I was smack in the middle of my menstrual cycle."

I turn to the plants, narrow my eyes, try to flee back into my madonna-in-the-hammock idyll. But the ferns stay ferns. What a crazy chance I took! I see a Dawson Construction cap stuck on Gray's head for good—no, for bad. Gray permanently stuck in the family business, paving over wilderness land, constructing shopping centers, condos, his wildlife-advocacy dreams down the drain, so he can support us. Or else us breaking up. Me on a table, feet in stirrups, not the riding kind, having an abortion. Having ruined everything. "Aren't you going to say something? Tell me I acted recklessly?"

Her face has stayed completely calm. She says, "I'm interested in why." She asks what birth control we use.

I tell her.

She asks, Did I ever not use it before, in the middle of my cycle?

"No."

"Then why, on Easter Sunday night?"

"Because it felt right. Like the perfect answer."

87

"To?"

"A whole lot of things."

"Like, for instance, to your mother's question, how serious you are about Gray?"

Serves me right; I shouldn't have told her! "Look, not everything has to do with my mother," I say scathingly. "What happened at the stables was strictly between Gray and me." I retreat into the corner of my chair.

In the car—Gray drove home—I wrapped the blanket around myself, tucked my feet under, scrunched myself up against his side, closed my eyes, and imagined us back into our wind-sheltered corner. It's a good technique I know, setting the stage for a dream I hope to have, planning the dream ahead of time, in some detail. I did that, and dropped off to sleep. I slept almost all the way back to the city. . . .

"It would be good if you could say what you are feeling."

Shh, no, it wouldn't. I'm trying to feel warm and snug, like in the car, dreaming all the way to the Triborough Bridge. When I woke up, I said, "Gray, you know what? I *did* have the greatest Easter. Did you?"

He said sweetly, Yes, he did.

"You know the part I liked best? After the horse neighed. When you said my name." I put my finger on his cheek. "You know what would be terrible?"

He stroked my hair and called me his darling in the same way he'd said my name. As if nobody in the world had ever said the word *darling* before.

We were stopped in a line of cars in front of the tolls

before crossing the East River into Manhattan. I felt safe and cozy. "If in the middle of, um, sex, you suddenly thought of somebody else. Did that ever happen to you?"

He smiled to himself.

"You don't have to tell me, if you don't want to."

He said, "That never happened to me with you. It's never going to."

The policeman in the tollbooth accepted our money. The light changed, and Gray drove on down the ramp, over into Manhattan. Recalling this part of the trip, I, the brave explorer of my secret self, make another discovery. Hey, Mom, you were right to wonder what your daughter's up to! My dream-producing technique that I bragged about so smugly just now blew a gasket, shredded up my blueprint; the dream took off on its own.

Dr. Schneck's antennae pick things up, even—especially?—during silences. "Did you just think of something startling?"

That's putting it mildly. I groan.

"Can you tell me about it?"

"The reason I don't like to drive at night is I worry about little animals on the road, running over one by accident. That's so dumb. *I* should have driven. Then I'd have had to stay awake. You see, I tried to dream a continuation of me and Gray, um, on the blanket." Music seeped in. The car radio was on. Some piano concerto was playing. The orchestra dropped out of the dream. The piano part kept on, improvising, smooth and slow and easy. Then it built, it swelled, to high, big waves. I sit up straight, rigid in the chair, to keep them from flowing back over me, flooding me right now.

"I don't think I told you," I say in an objective tone. "When Gray and Joe were freshmen, they were matched up as roommates probably through some computer error, because their backgrounds are as different as can be. Well, instead of ignoring or disliking each other, as roommates often do, they hit it off just fine, became close friends." My voice has gone down to a whisper. "One kind of person I despise . . ."

She can't hear. "Please speak a little louder."

"One kind of person I despise is a friendship wrecker." I cover my face with my hands.

"What happened in the dream?"

"Oh, it was great. The only trouble is, the person on the blanket with me turned into Joe."

She asks me to uncover my face. She says, "You are taking the dream at its literal level, and condemning yourself with it. You are being a very stern judge. Perhaps next time we will have a chance to see why."

VIII

Thursday, April 28, 4:20–5:10 P.M.

What am I doing here? I feel as out of place in this
quiet, sheltered room as my sky-blue Nikes look garish
on her muted rug.

"How are you feeling today?"

"Healthy. Guilty. Oh, what's the difference?" Eleven
blocks down and across town from here's a hospital full
of people really sick. Not just tense and tight as I am,
muscles stiff, jaw clenched, sitting here. I shift my gaze
from floor to ceiling, peruse the shelves, starting from
the top. I'd rather read every title and author of every
book, examine every ornament, study each of the eight

framed diplomas and certificates, than meet her unperturbable gaze.

"You seem unhappy," those diplomas attesting to her erudition enable her to guess.

"I am. And ashamed."

"Of what?"

"Throwing away Dad's money on sitting here, finding things out that I'd rather not know."

"What things?"

"*You* know. My dream, in the car. What a bummer. I was all happy, all proud of myself, telling you about Gray and me, that it was good, finally. I thought *you* were pleased that I could tell it to you so directly. Everything was hunky-dory. Then, wham! Dreams are your secret wishes, isn't that what psychiatrists think? Well, it should have stayed secret, I'd be better off."

She says, "You underestimate dreams. They don't yield up their meanings quite so easily. They do contain wishes, certainly. But you can't understand the wishes without associating to the dream, telling all that occurs to you about it, and following the paths the associations lead you in, regardless how far afield some of those paths may seem to go."

"My dream wasn't that complicated. I already know what it means."

"Yes? What does it mean?"

"I'm screwing up my life!"

"Tell me how."

I start with my fight with Gray. Yesterday after Art History I went over there. Clack, clack, he was typing

92

away, writing up a section of his project on Belinda that his adviser, Mr. Mackleson, had asked to see.

The place is reasonably neat, usually. Well, it was a mess, books and papers strewn around, the Futon not folded up, a few items of clothes on the floor. And Gray hadn't shaved. His hair was tousled—the way I like it. He had his oldest jeans on, and an undershirt left over from his childhood, with more holes than shirt to it.

He went straight back to typing after letting me in. I leaned over and hugged him.

"Hey, you made me make a mistake."

"Not a serious one, I hope. Listen, I need help with my biology."

He pressed his head against my middle. "Your biology seems okay to me." He took one moment out for kissing, then typed on, double speed.

I started to pick things up off the floor, stuffed a shirt and a sock into the bottom drawer of his bureau where he keeps clothes to be washed.

"Don't. I'll take care of that later. See if Bart's hungry, would you?"

Bartram's head was buried in the sand of his cage. He was fast asleep.

"If you really want to help, cross check these figures for me." He handed me some index cards with data and some typed pages with the same data in charts comparing Belinda's fish consumption and weight gain from December to February.

I sat down across from him, turned the radio on.

"Turn that down; I can't concentrate."

So I went and worked in the kitchen.

After a while he came in there. "Sorry I'm edgy. Mackleson has office hours till six. I said I'd bring this section over before then. How about if I fix us some tea?"

He poured his in a mug and paced around with it. He's nervous over when Belinda will go into labor. He picked up the phone, called Phil at the aquarium. Phil said nothing new.

It could start anytime now. Then again, it might not for another few weeks. Nobody knows exactly.

Gray made a deal with his father: In exchange for his father not bugging him about refusing to go into the business permanently, Gray would work this whole summer for Dawson Construction, starting as soon after graduation as he can get home, and he's not going by plane. He has so much stuff, he's going to rent a U-Haul and drive. The idea that Belinda might delay giving birth till after he has left is driving him mad.

I said, "Relax, you'll get your magna, whether you're around for the delivery or not."

"I don't give one hoot in hell about what honors I get, and you know it."

"I know. Sorry. Sit with me a minute."

"I don't have time."

"Mackleson can wait. What do you need his comments for, at this point, anyway? You know more about it than he does. He's never even seen a pregnant beluga."

"He's seen plenty of senior projects, though. Look, I just have to get this done." He started through the swinging door.

"Just one minute?" I wheedled in a way I didn't like.

He went on through. I raised my voice. "Belinda may not be the only pregnant female in your life!"

He came back in the kitchen.

I said, "Remember Easter Sunday?"

"You said it was safe."

"Well, it wasn't. I'm sorry to lay this on you when you're so pushed for time."

He came up behind me, the way I'd done to him before, tilted my head back, and gave me his crooked-toothed grin. I flung my arms around him. What I was after, the real reason I'd come, was to find this out: Had my last session with Dr. Schneck destroyed our Easter-Sunday-night magic? Or could we reinvoke it? I put my hand through a big hole in his T-shirt, ran my hand up lightly over the hairs on his chest. "Last time was so good," I said in a sultry voice, "I couldn't bear for it to stop." I gave him a long look.

He misread it. He thought I was still apologizing that I'd told him it was safe. He kissed me on the forehead. "Don't worry. Getting knocked up from one glorious, careless rapture happens more often in romantic novels than in real life," and went back to pounding his Smith-Corona.

I turned the radio way up. The kitchen filled with riffs and runs up and down the keyboard, jazz piano, the kind Joe strives for like a distant goal when he practices on the tinny upright in his room. I tried to tap my foot to it, coolly, nonchalantly, but the beat was unpredictable. I waited for the set to end, for Joe to announce who'd been playing. But an unfamiliar voice came on. "The last number you heard was, bla, bla—"

I burst out of the kitchen. "Gray, how come somebody else is doing Joe's show?"

"Take it easy!" Gray ripped the page out of the machine, crumpled it to show I'd made him mess it up. "Lucky fell again. Joe made him an appointment with a doctor. Then he thought Lucky wouldn't keep it unless he went with him."

"How come you didn't tell me?"

"It's not a big crisis. Relax."

"What kind of doctor?"

"I don't know. His name's Fischer. His office is at Roosevelt Hospital. Now can I go back and do this?"

"You don't think anything's a crisis unless it weighs a zillion pounds and has a melon on its forehead!"

I went over to Bartram. He was looking around in his glass cage, flicking his pretty pink tongue. I went and took him out. He started to wind himself around my arm. "No, I don't need you for a bracelet just now."

Gray put a fresh sheet of paper in the typewriter. "Here, feed him yourself." I draped Bartram around his shoulders. "So long." I grabbed my raincoat, books, and I left. I took the bus down to Roosevelt.

Working harder than usual at avoiding Dr. Schneck's face, I tell this story to the various objects in the room.

On her desk is a vase of irises, the box of Kleenex at the edge (so she can reach it without getting up), and a large black tooled-leather mat. On this mat is something white. An envelope. I don't know precisely at what moment of the session I become aware of it.

96

"Joe's uncle was admitted to the hospital. He's going to have some tests . . ."

In the middle of saying this, I imagine a Mr. Schneck, white-haired, dapper, distinguished-looking, sitting opposite Dr. Schneck at dinner, and Dr. Schneck telling him, in glowing terms, I have an extraordinarily altruistic young patient, so concerned with other people. . . . No, on second thought, I don't want her telling anybody about me, even to sing my praises. In my mind I move her to behind her desk, writing—a note to herself about my admirable concern for the health of the uncle of a friend? No, to me, *Dear Ms. Moskowitz* . . . No. *Dear Dinah* . . . I have her put her pen to her chin while she ponders how to word her keen appreciation of me, both as a patient and a person. . . .

"What sort of tests?" she asks.

"I don't know what they're called. You probably think I'm a phony."

"Why?"

"Well, rushing off to check on Lucky was also a way of showing I was mad at Gray, of getting even with him. Lucky's not someone that close to me. But I *am* concerned, for him, and because Joe's so concerned. He's closer to Lucky than to either of his parents."

The bed by the door was vacant. Lucky sat up in the one by the window looking like a handsomer, older, solider variation of Joe. He blew a perfect smoke ring at the sign on the wall of a cigarette with a big red X drawn through it. He flirted with me in his gentle, easy way, said though I was the cheeriest sight he'd seen in many hours, he couldn't flatter himself into believing the only reason I'd come was to visit *him*.

I made a point of staying, chatting.

"Go on, now. You've kept this broken-down old piano player company long enough," he said after a while. "You'll find Joe in the lounge."

When I got there, though, I almost didn't see him. He was sitting on a vinyl love seat, wrapped in a dense cloud of smoke. He was watching TV, which would have been okay, except the set wasn't on.

The thing is, he'd seriously quit smoking on New Year's Eve, and had stayed clean except that one time when Carole stood him up.

I sat down, leaving as much vinyl-covered space between us as possible.

Joe told me the situation: Lucky's right leg is numb. A cut on the big toe isn't healing. If it doesn't soon, it may get gangrenous. Not enough blood is circulating to the foot. Dr. Fischer thinks he's got Burger's disease, a clogging of the arteries. Believe it or not, one cause of Burger's Disease is eating rye bread—which Lucky never touches. The other cause is smoking cigarettes.

As a zinger to the story, Joe lit another Marlboro. "I know, I know. I'm only smoking this one pack."

"*Why?*"

"So the pleasure will be fresh in my mind. So I won't act like a sanctimonious prig about it when I make him quit. Because if I don't make him, who will?"

It's hard to explain this, but *I* took one from the pack. I lit it from the burning end of Joe's. I've smoked cigarettes before, but not regularly. I never liked the taste too much; it always made my throat feel scratchy. This time I took the smoke in deep, and imagined how it felt to Joe. I held the smoke in my lungs till it felt good in there. When I finally breathed it out, through my nostrils, it mingled in the air with the smoke Joe had exhaled. I watched the bluish wisps and smoke plumes rise and waft around, drift apart, merge back together, give momentary shape to Joe's feelings, my feelings. Heady stuff! I started to take another drag.

He took the cigarette out of my mouth.

Across from us sat a man in a hospital gown, so sick he was rigged to an intravenous bottle from which fluid dripped into a vein in his arm. Upstairs from us, in operating rooms, surgeons were busy doing dangerous things to organs inside people's bodies. All around us, on every floor, in every room of that huge hospital, people were in pain, some dying that very moment—while my entire consciousness was taken up with the sensation of Joe's index finger brushing against my lips.

He stubbed the cigarette out in the ashtray.

I tell this story, interspersed with silences, to Dr. Schneck's books, *Sexual Identity,* by Green, to *On the Nightmare,* by Jones. I tell it to a four-inch tall Egyptian cat smiling down from between the books. Thanks, I'm glad to get a smile, even a miniature bronze one. I tell it to the pictures, diplomas, and certificates, to the heavy dark blue ashtray on the end table behind the couch. Does anybody stub out cigarettes in it? I tell it to my old friends, the Levolors, to the plants, to the desk, the black tooled-leather desk mat. . . . What's in that envelope?

She asks me why looking her in the face today seems to be particularly troubling.

The handwriting on the envelope is small and even.

She asks, Am I afraid that she would look as if she didn't understand me, or as if she disapproved?

"I don't know. Both. *I* don't even understand. And *I* disapprove."

"Of your feelings for Joe?"

"Yes. They're like in the dream. I'm scared." I start to cry.

I need a Kleenex badly, reach for one, and read—or do I just imagine?—my name on the envelope that's lying on the mat.

I close my eyes.

"Where are you in your thoughts?"

"Ashcroft." I can't help it! "Why does that summer feel as if it's still going on?"

"Perhaps because you were trying to make choices then, as you are trying to do now."

I don't know. . . . "No, I'm not 'trying' now, I've *made* them." But there's more immediacy to standing in the flagpole field than sitting in this chair. Standing in a circle for mail call. Mrs. Herbert reads out the names. Moskowitz came after Minz, Muller after Moskowitz. She never went right from Minz to Muller. I always got mail. Dad wrote me little notes all the time, put them in separate envelopes, so there'd be more for me to open. He and Mom had an agreement that they weren't going to try to influence me. He'd been ignoring it right along.

The theme of all his notes to me was, How much I'd love New York. *Dear Dinah, Guess what kind of store opened up, right in this apartment building—a kite store. Guess what else: Directly across from this apartment lives a girl who I bet is just your age; you two can get to know each other, waving out the window. . . .*

Other people write me too: Ellen Steinfeld, my grandparents, and I even got two cards from Ricky Sturges.

And of course Mom wrote me letters from Arizona. My counselor, Marsha Derwent, an anthropology major at U. Mass., loved Mom's letters. She copied out parts about the dig, and about the Hopi Indians. All that information would come in handy when she went back to school. She made me read one letter aloud at a campfire. It was about a ceremonial dance Mom had gotten permission to observe.

Mom's handwriting is angular and slanty. I used to practice imitating it. I wanted to write just like that. I didn't know yet that handwriting is like fingerprints and snowflakes. No matter what you do, no two handwritings are exactly alike. It'll always be just your own.

"Dearest Dinah," I practiced writing to myself with Mom's sharp down-thrust *D*'s and up-slanting *T* cross, one rainy afternoon in the Rec Hall at Ashcroft when we were supposed to write letters *to* our parents.

I tell this anecdote. I try to sound amused at the childish pastime.

"What was in the letter to yourself?"

"I don't know. I don't remember anymore."

At the end of the session, she hands me the envelope that's been lying on the desk. In it is my bill for April.

IX

Monday, May 2, 3:40–4:30 P.M.

What am I supposed to do, go right up to her, hand her the check? I haven't got the courage. Slip it in the pocket of her cardigan? That would be incredibly gauche. Lay it facedown on her desk? That would be less awkward. But I can't, I just can't! I'll wait till after. I'll do it when I leave.

I avoid her hello smile, sit down.

She says, "You seem uncomfortable." Another understatement of the year!

Paying her's just like . . . I can't even put the thought into words to myself. If I were following the rules, playing fair, I'd have to say it. I could sooner quote the lurid graffiti a filthy-minded subway rider wrote all over the Calvin Klein jeans ad in the 116th Street station.

"Why are you so uncomfortable?" she asks.

"Because I thought of something I can't possibly say to you, no matter how much you'd assure me that it would be all right. And because I know that no matter what all else I do say, I'll be thinking of it this whole session."

Out of her large repertoire of variations on a smile, she gives me one that says, Of course it would be better if I *could* say it, but okay, she understands.

"I should get a job. Wash dishes, waitress, work at one of the libraries at school. Anything, so I could start repaying Dad. . . ." He was good, didn't wince, didn't ask, am I making progress, getting anywhere with this, just wrote out the check.

"I shouldn't go to London. I'll just be spending more of his money. I wish I could get out of it." I feel hot, gather my hair up, hold it away from my neck. "*You* say something now."

She leans forward. Her glasses are up in her hair. The green cardigan brings out her eyes. Also, I think she must have gotten some fresh air; she has more color in her face. Anyway, somehow she seems younger. She asks, "What do you wish I would say?"

"I don't know." I'd know it if I heard it! I don't know what to talk about. I go on, about London. "Dad's been making arrangements, ordering tickets to plays and things. And Audrey's trying really hard to win me over. She bounced into my room last night—I was trying to study for finals—and listed all the tourist places she wants us to go see. Buckingham Palace, the Tower, London Bridge—wait till she finds out it's been moved to someplace here in America."

I feel bitchy talking about Audrey like that. I switch to Lucky. "He's going to have an arteriogram. That's supposed to be painful. He's acting cheerful, though. I feel super self-indulgent, sitting here, healthy as a horse, telling you my overprivileged problems. . . ." At sixty-five dollars per, which brings me back full-circle to Thought A.

"I'm thirsty. I shouldn't have put so much hot mustard on my hot dog at lunch." Julie's shrink doesn't charge extra for the coffee or tea. And she charges—only!—fifty dollars.

My face feels about to burst into flame.

"I didn't get my period yesterday. I'm usually regular as clockwork." The African violet's blooming its heart out, purple and lush. The ferns stand nice and tall. Too bad my Everglades mother-and-child fantasy doesn't work anymore. "I feel lousy about everything. Gray's busy the whole week. I won't see him till Friday. Not even then, if Belinda goes into labor, which is all he thinks about." I braid my hair, unbraid it. "Sorry you have to listen to all this self-pity. I like your little cat up there.

"*I* had a cat, when I was little. Her name was Butterscotch. One night Mom was reading to me in front of our fireplace. Everything was cozy, like in a picture book. Then a car pulled into our driveway. A man came to the door. He wore a raincoat. It bulged. Something was hidden underneath. Something dark—blood

—seeped through. 'Go upstairs,' Mom told me. But I'd seen.

"Well, at least he wasn't a hit-and-run driver.

"I wrote my cat a letter. I addressed it to Butterscotch Moskowitz, c/o Cat Heaven. I didn't believe in a cat heaven. But I could imagine such a place, and I couldn't imagine death. It didn't sink in that I'd never see her again."

Dr. Schneck says, "You felt bereaved."

I squirm. "Don't feel sorry for me!" I feel under false pretenses, telling pitiful stories, all the while thinking unsayable things.

She says, "You are giving yourself a very hard time."

No denying that.

"It wasn't even dark yet when he ran her over. So that can't have anything to do with why I don't like to drive at night. I don't know. Darkness does increase your chances of hitting some little animal. It happens a lot. You see squirrels, raccoons, woodchucks on the roadsides pretty often; it's no big deal."

Dr. Schneck says, "I have the impression that when you use this phrase, 'no big deal,' you are covering over some very strong feelings."

I try to remember when I used it before.

What I do remember, sharply: An opossum, eyes glowing, like little green flashlights in the night. One time, as I was taking the garbage out, I saw one, in back of the house, standing still, not seeming afraid, just calmly watching, a mama opposum with three babies on her back. . . .

But that's not the one. The one I remember—"no

big deal"—lay belly-up, guts exposed, on the roadside. Two crows stood over it, with their beaks in its flesh. I tell this to Dr. Schneck.

She asks, "Is this something you actually saw?"

"Yes."

"When?"

"The winter I was in sixth grade. On the way to riding. It was Mom's last year at Sarah Lawrence. She went there Mondays, Wednesdays, and Fridays. Monday was my riding day. Usually a high-school senior who lived near us, Vicky Crawford, drove me. But when I came home from school that afternoon, instead of Vicky's old blue Plymouth in the driveway, there stood Mom's new red Datsun, blazing in the snow. She'd just gotten it. 'Di-zey, surprise!' Mom called out the upstairs bathroom window. 'I'm playing hooky; I'll drive you today.'

"Great! I wore my not-yet-broken-in new riding boots and hat just to look good. I was thrilled.

"I hadn't gone anywhere in the Datsun yet. Mom let me put the key in the ignition. I turned the motor on. She showed me how to put the car in drive. 'Now give it a little gas, press down with your foot, easy. Again, a little more. Now let it coast.' She let me drive it as far as the road. She said I did fine; I'd make a good driver.

"I made her go past Ricky Sturges's house. I was crazy about him. He was older, in junior high already. I reached over Mom and honked the horn so he'd see us. He quit shooting baskets long enough to yell, 'Neat car!' I was in heaven.

106

"It was a January thaw day, almost balmy. Icicles dripped from roofs and porches of houses we passed. The sky was bright blue and white clouds piled up in the west like snow-covered mountains.

"I turned on the radio. I just knew something would be playing that would match my mood. Joni Mitchell came on, singing 'Both Sides Now.' She was my favorite singer. She sounded more like a regular person than somebody who got paid to sing. She shifts registers a lot, like Mom does. My mother has a beautiful voice, only she can't carry a tune. She's self-conscious about it. She never sings around other people. When she was a little girl, she had to, in church, and people would tell her she was off pitch. I loved that about her. I mean, that there was something she didn't do well. And that she'd do it in front of me. Anyhow, in the car, she sang along with Joni, going way off pitch, and so did I, just to keep her company, '. . . I've looked at clouds from both sides now, from up and down . . .'

"When I was five, flying out to Wichita, Kansas, to visit Mom's parents, I really did see clouds 'from up'— the tops of clouds, through the airplane window. It was so amazing! They were like the backs of a million giant woolly sky-sheep.

"I wished I were going somewhere in an airplane again. I thought of Mom taking a plane out to Arizona, to that dig. She was looking forward to it a lot.

"And I thought of Dad's Whooshy commercial. He'd just started doing it around that time. The baby in the Whooshy disposable diaper floats on top of clouds too.

Anyway, I had babies on the brain that winter, because of my friend Ellen. She was about to stop being the only other only child in the neighborhood. I was going to be the only only child left. Mrs. Steinfeld, Ellen's mom, was pregnant.

"When the cloud song was over, I asked Mom if she envied Mrs. Steinfeld."

I feel a twinge of cramps.

"Mom said No, talked about other things."

I don't have a Tampax on me. Thinking of blood. . . .

"Suddenly Mom swerved out to the middle of the road. There was this dead opossum lying on the side. I looked away. I wasn't that squeamish. I just didn't want the sight of it to jinx my afternoon.

"The riding was great. We got Janice, the nicer, less sarcastic of the two instructors who alternated taking our group. She let me take Cherokee. He acted glad to see me, snorted hello, lowered his head for me to pet his sleek brown cheeks.

"We went on the long trail, down the dirt road through woods, across a sunny, open stubble field. A flock of robins swooped past. Some of them stay around Connecticut the whole winter. Even so, seeing them made it feel like spring.

"On the way back, Janice said, 'The more advanced of you may gallop. Dinah, you too.' I loosened up on the reins, pressed my heels against Cherokee's sides. He spurted forward. First I sat tight. Then I got more confident. I stood up in the stirrups, crouched forward, leaned over his neck, the way I'd seen jockeys do on

108

TV. His hooves barely touched the ground. I felt as if my three years of riding lessons, all the spills, all the nasty cracks from the other instructors, had been worth it, were finally paying off. The wind roared past, like music that hadn't been composed yet, that only Cherokee and I could hear. It was like galloping through the air. It was the best ride I'd ever had.

"Mom had sat in the car, studying, the whole time.

" 'Mom, listen, I have this terrific idea: How about if we build a stall onto the back of our garage? It wouldn't have to be expensive. I could do some of it myself, and we could take in a horse to board; that way I could ride all I want.'

"She let me go on about it, didn't say what a harebrained scheme it was, just waited till I was through. Then she said she had something to tell me.

"Part of me thirsted for some terrible disaster. I don't know why. Maybe everybody has a disaster-thirsty part to them. The rest of me didn't want to hear it.

"We were coming to the opossum. It was less than a mile away. I remember being silent."

I'm silent now too, in this psychotherapeutic chair. I wondered (I'd been reading a fair amount of science fiction that year) if, by some ultimate-math method, time could spiral, or gyrate, in a way that could cause the little red Datsun, with the two of us in it, to travel for eons, for all eternity, along that short stretch of road edged with winter-dead grass and bare, straggly bushes. . . .

"Your mother had something to tell you," Dr.

Schneck recapitulates. Her voice sounds far away to me.

I think she senses this. She moves forward as far as she can and says into my silence, "I wonder, when you wished that I would say something, was it that I would urge you not to go to London? Urge you instead to keep coming here, to me?"

You shrinks are all alike, I want to say. You're a bunch of egomaniacs. You don't really care what the person in the other chair is going through. You're just thinking of yourself, how important *you* are! The thing that makes it worse is, she happens to be right.

My neck protests, it makes a crackling noise when I bend it to nod my head. My right shoulder aches. All this time it's been hunched up as high as my ear. I lower it. I want to laugh lightly and dismissingly. I say, but it comes out a groan, "Yes, I wished that." And out comes what I've been harboring this entire session: "Paying money for this is like paying a prostitute."

She's wearing a blouse that has a little lace collar, with a cameo pin on it like one my Grandma Ida has. Her throat is crepe-paper delicate. She's fragile, she's old, she's refined. I feel monstrous having said that to her. But I don't retreat. "It's just the same, paying for sex, or for somebody's attention. Paying money for such things invalidates the entire process." I sound remarkably detached, considering the turmoil in me. I feel like the little girl out of whose mouth hop poisonous toads in a horrible Andersen story.

Dr. Schneck is utterly unruffled. She stands. "Perhaps next time—"

Before she even finishes the sentence, I leap to my feet and dash out.

Halfway through the short passage to the waiting room, I whack myself on the forehead. Stupid! I have to go back in.

I forgot to give her the check. I nearly took it back home with me. I put it on her desk and flee.

X

Thursday, May 5, 4:20–5:10 P.M.

If somebody'd compared *me* to a prostitute, I doubt I could welcome that person with such a calm, friendly *hello.*

"I've been thinking about what I said. About people paying you money. I'm incredibly embarrassed. Of course you have to get paid, or how could you live? And then I nearly walked out of here with the check still in my wallet!" I laugh, repeat the whack on the forehead.

"It was not a joking matter to you. You had strong feelings about it."

"I know. I didn't want to pay you, obviously."

"Can you tell me more about that?"

"I guess I don't want to be 'people.' I don't want to be just another patient." I say this coolly, with detachment, as if I were talking about somebody else. "I guess I want to be special. Someone you'd *want* to see. So much that you'd do it for free."

"You sound self-mocking."

"I do? I guess because it's laughable."

She answers with utter gravity, "It is not laughable."

I know. I really agree. I need to get off this subject before it spoils my mood of relief and of things going well. I tell her, "I got my period. As soon as I left here on Monday. I had a feeling, during the session, that it was coming on."

Good, I called up Gray. We'd laugh about it, he'd see that I was over being angry with him. He wasn't home. I called the aquarium, got Phil d'Alessandro. Phil said Gray was busy with Belinda (in his wet suit, in the belugas' pool; they keep it at an invigorating 53 degrees). Phil asked, "Can I give him a message?"

"Tell him to call me if he gets a chance."

I felt like talking to somebody. I called Mom. Nadia answered; Mom wasn't home yet. I tried calling her office at Wesleyan. But she'd already left.

No luck with Julie either. She's going out to visit her father and his California family right after graduation. She's on an all-out instant-thinness quest in preparation for the trip. She couldn't talk; she had to rush to aerobics.

Okay, well, I'd study. The old habit of grinding away for A's and B-pluses got the better of me. Even though it won't make an iota of difference down in the Everglades what grades I got this term. All I have to do is pass, which I can, without cracking a book.

I lost myself a little while in the Garden of Eden of *Paradise Lost.* I skimmed through the anthropology reading. The rah-rah tone—hey, students, this is an exciting field—got my goat again.

I wished somebody would call me.

Somebody did. Audrey. She and Dad were going to a screening, she could wangle me an invitation, would I like to join them?

"Thanks, really, a lot, Audrey; that's nice of you. But I have to study."

I wandered out on the terrace, watched the people go by.

One time, the first September I lived here, Julie and I stood leaning over the railing, dropping down Baggies filled with water, fastened with plastic ties. It was a very hot day. We were being rain goddesses, granting aid to the poor parched pavement, and to a surprised passer-by or two.

Well, pretty soon a policeman came up and gave us a severe talking-to but didn't tell Dad.

Julie met my then big requirements for a friend: living nearby and having divorced parents. Her father's a conductor-composer. He'd just remarried and moved to the West Coast. Julie hadn't met his new wife and children yet. She missed him passionately and had daily battles with her mom. After them she'd come over, and we'd have marathon heart-to-hearts about the unfairness of parents' custody fights. She hated living with her mother. We'd work out wonderful scenarios whereby her father could have her kidnapped and spirited away.

I tell all this to Dr. Schneck and vividly remember basking in Julie's undisguised envy of me that I was living with my dad.

On the terrace our lilies of the valley are in bloom. Dad started them the first year we lived here. They do almost as well in big wooden planters as under the lilac bush in back of our house in Rowayton.

I picked a bunch, brought them in, looked for a vase. No, changed my mind. On an impulse, took them to the hospital.

I truly didn't expect to run into Joe. Joe has a seminar in Constitutional History on Mondays at five. His professor had warned him: no more cuts or no credit for the term.

Well, but when I got to Roosevelt, there he was, just leaving, loping toward me, awful posture, slouching worse than ever, eyes cast down, glaring at the polished hospital lobby floor as if it were his enemy, about to spit in his eye.

Next time I need a boost to my self-confidence I'll think of the way his face lit up, like all the lights coming back on after a blackout, when he caught sight of me.

He was in a rage at Lucky. He'd found a pack of Winstons hidden under his pillow. Lucky needed a kick where it would hurt the most, not a bunch of lilies of the valley. "But go ahead up. I'll wait here for you."

Lucky put a sprig in his pajama top lapel, said the scent brought back his young years in Chicago and girls he'd known who'd smelled not half so sweet.

He flirted charmingly with me in a low voice, because the other bed was occupied by a very sick-looking old man. Almost whispering, he sang me the opening of his latest composition; in fact, he was still working on it in his head. He called it the "Waiting-for-Your-Bypass Rag."

Joe'd brought him a Walkman so he could listen to music without disturbing the other patient. "Walkman, that beats Wheelchair-man, or Flat-on-my-can man—sorry, poor taste."

I said, Fine. Anybody who has to have an operation was automatically entitled to behave in the poorest imaginable taste.

He said, "Sit a minute." He's worried about Joe neglecting his schoolwork. He took my hand, held it in both of his. It's not true that all pianists have sensitive, long fingers. His are squat with little dark hairs growing on the fleshy part behind the knuckles. Those little ugly hairs really got to me. They made me think of the blood flowing underneath that's supposed to keep everything going and growing, blood flowing all through the body, through a complicated maze of veins and arteries—with which a bunch of doctors are going to interfere. I just hoped those doctors knew their business and had good, steady hands.

Lucky said, "Promise you won't let Joe louse himself up and not graduate on account of worrying about me." He thinks I have some power over him.

I didn't argue with that. I said I'd try.

He lifted up his pillow. He opened the drawer of the cabinet beside the bed, where he keeps his toothbrush and shaving stuff. "See? I'm clean, no more cigarettes. I'm really quitting. Scout's honor." He grinned, just with his mouth. His eyes, deep, dark brown like Joe's, were serious.

"Oh, sure," Joe said cynically when I told him. "Just like Mark Twain; he quit a few times every day. You should have heard the sermon I preached at him. If Northwestern Law takes back my acceptance once they see my final grades, I can always get a job as browbeater with one of those quit-smoking outfits people pay big money to."

"What was the sermon?"

"Oh, that he's wasting a good hospital bed, and the nurses' and doctors' time, and his and mine. I told him, Forget the bypass, forget about his good other leg, too, it won't stay good for long with cigarette smoke clogging up the blood flow to it, forget the whole thing. So long, it was good to know him."

I put my arm around Joe. If the ERA ever gets passed, it better have a clause lifting the ban, unwritten but powerful, on men crying. They ought to be able to, like everybody else.

"Come on, let's get out of here." I navigated him through the dismal lobby full of scared, defeated-looking people, through the revolving door into the early-evening sunshine.

He was starving. So was I. There's a greasy luncheonette on the next corner. He wanted to go and have hamburgers there.

"I know where you can get better ones."

Home. I made us some with everything on them:

cheddar cheese, mushrooms, onions, tomato, and ketch-up. Joe said, Great. He wolfed his down. I don't think he tasted it that much. He was even hungrier for talking.

"Dinah, what'll I do if he dies?

"You can't imagine how great Lucky's always been to me." When Joe was a little kid, if it hadn't been for Lucky, his life would have been a drag. He took him to all the good places, parades, the circus, White Sox games. Lucky taught him to swim in Lake Michigan, did all the things Joe's "legal-eagle" parents were too busy to even think about.

Lucky had a jazz quintet in those days, let Joe hang around during practice sessions, let him fool around on the piano, gave him his whole love for music.

Damn it, Joe'd felt like shouting at him, all he really loved were Winstons, more than his life, "more than me! *Lucky loved Winstons.* That can be the inscription on his gravestone." Joe tapped the words out in frenetic rhythm on the wooden tabletop. "Dinah, I'm scared. Not just for him, for myself. What if I lose the guy? And he worries about me doing my schoolwork! Why? So I can be a good little law student like my parents ordered and grow up to be a fat-cat lawyer, wear suits from J. Press and Gucci shoes, spend my life sniffing out tax loopholes for corporations?"

"Joe, there's other kinds of lawyers."

"Sure, I know. I just can't care about that now." He stood up, paced around, opened a cabinet drawer. It so happened, it was our catch-all drawer, where we keep things like toothpicks, cocktail napkins, Velamints, gum. He rummaged in there, came up with a pack of matches. Was there, by chance, anything at all to smoke, anywhere in the apartment? A longish butt would be okay.

No, it wouldn't. Anyway, there wasn't one, so I didn't have the problem of withholding it from him.

The coffee was ready. I poured him a cup. "Come on, sit here; drum on the table some more."

I didn't know my voice could sound so soothing. I gave him some ice cream. His left hand was lying on the table, skinny fingers, same little dark hairs behind the knuckles; ugly, I suppose. But I thought of the blood flowing under there, young and strong, nothing in its way. I worried about Lucky, sure. But still, I felt this rush of happiness that Joe was sitting there with me. I put my hand over his. His didn't move, just raised up a tiny bit, to acknowledge, welcome mine. I thought, without any embarrassment, that our two hands on the tabletop looked like two animals of some undiscovered species getting together, mating.

I'm hardly ever in our kitchen when some ambulance doesn't screech past, down Lexington, on its way to Lenox Hill Hospital. For once this didn't happen. I'd lowered the blinds—we have Levolors too, only they're white—to keep out the glare of the sun going down. It was quiet and peaceful.

Then the bell rang. We went to the door. There stood Gray. I was thrilled as always when I don't expect to see him. I also had a pang, wondering what he'd think seeing Joe there with me. He said, "I called you back but you were out."

"I went over to the hospital. I ran into Joe."

"And brought me back for hamburgers and sympathy," said Joe.

"Want one?" I asked.

Gray said, "Sure." He pulled me to him, held me. "Guess what I was doing when I couldn't come to the phone? Putting this gizmo, an electronic stethoscope, to Belinda's belly. She didn't even mind. This may not sound too strictly scientific, but I think she could sense what it was about. I mean, she knows, or senses, that there's a whale baby in there. Fetus, I mean. I heard its heart beat! Like this." He put his mouth to my ear, made bursts of sound from way deep in his throat: pum, pum, pum.

The three of us went into the kitchen.

While I was melting the cheddar on top of the meat, the phone rang.

"Dinah, hi. Nadia said you called. What's up?"

"Hi, Mom. Nothing special. I just felt like talking. I can't now; I'm cooking something. I've got company."

She didn't ask, I didn't have to say who. I stood with my back to the refrigerator, got a great lift out of thinking, Hey, it's an inoffensive white G.E. Not avocado color, not a Coldspot! Seeing Gray and Joe sitting side by side gave me another rush of happiness like before, double strength. Besides, I'd gotten my period, that also had something to do with feeling so at ease, so okay. I didn't have to prove anything to anybody! I said, "Mom, Gray and Joe are here just now. Are you home? Can I call you later?"

Mom said that would be fine.

Between Gray and me, we calmed Joe down, got him

to agree that Lucky had a good chance. Then the two of us lit into him about school. Gray made him promise he'd go see the Constitutional Law professor, see if he could make up for cutting class, do everything humanly possible to make sure he graduated.

"Don't you go bugging out on me, hear?" Gray puffed out his chest. "When I'm an important (*im-poh-tant*) advocate for wildlife, I'm going to need me a powerful environmentalist lawyer. That better be you, old buddy." He laid on the drawl, heavy and slow, and had us all laughing good and loud. I don't know when I felt as close to two people as I did that evening, and it was mutual, three ways.

When we'd polished off two pints of ice cream, one vanilla Häagen-Dazs, one chocolate Alpen Zauber, a package of Lido cookies, and most of a package of Milanos, Gray said he was fading, had to go home to catch up on sleep.

Joe offered to do the dishes. "So you guys can say good night."

We went into my room. We lay down on my bed together. I told Gray my period came. He was glad, though he hadn't been worried.

I sum this up increasingly breathlessly as the session rushes by.

"We kissed good night. In the language of kisses, it said everything was fine between us.

"I was sure I'd sleep really well. But then I had this dream."

"Can you tell me about it?"

"I'd rather not. I'd rather get back to where I left off

the last time. I feel driven to get back to that." Driven, ha, ha, like in the Datsun. I didn't make the joke on purpose, it just came out that way. I'd laugh, but my mood has changed.

Dr. Schneck says, "Of course, you must talk about whatever you most need to."

Now that I brought up the dream, I find I can't *not* tell it. "I was walking down a road. There were tall trees on either side. It looked like Riverside Drive. I was with Gray. We were walking next to each other, carefully not touching, not even just our fingertips. It was terribly important. Not to look at each other, either. Well, I couldn't stop myself. I stole a look up at his face. And I saw these fat tears running down it. He was wearing his red cableknit sweater, that his grandmother made for him, and it was getting wet. Teardrops stuck to the shoulders, like glass beads. It was my fault he was crying. I'd done something to him. When I woke up, the dream felt as if it had actually happened. It still does."

Only four more minutes. "Look, I have to do all these normal things this weekend: Stay over at my aunt and uncle's; they're going away, and I volunteered to take care of Jonathan. And I said I'd go see Belinda. I want to be fun when I do those things, not act like a zombie, all gloomy. But I don't see how I can! I'll be thinking all the time about the place I left off. *You* know. Mom and me, driving home from the stables."

I sway back and forward in my chair. "After we passed the opossum. When I couldn't see its carcass out the back window anymore. Mom said—"

My watch says the session's over.

122

Dr. Schneck's still seated though.

"She and Dad were getting divorced. So what? Big deal! So many of my friends' parents had already done that. It was almost more unusual if your parents stayed married." My shoulder throbs. I can hear every breath whistling faintly up my nose as I breathe the air in, and huff as it goes out.

"How did you feel?" asks Dr. Schneck.

"Okay. Blank."

"What do you feel about it now?"

"Nothing."

Nothing weighs zero. How come it's so hard to hoist myself up out of this chair?

"Wait just a minute, please. If you like, I could see you tomorrow, at three."

I have Biology lab, but I'm caught up; I can miss it. A ton of weight drops off me. "Yes."

XI

"Those two brats were in the elevator again, bubble gum and all. I thought, Good, this'll confuse them. 'Hey, it's Friday, what's *she* doing here?' was written all over their faces. It threw off their whole system of keeping tabs on your patients." I laugh. "I'm really glad I'm having this extra session. I'm really going to use it, not waste any time." I go directly to where I left off:

"In the Datsun, feet tucked under me on the red upholstered front seat, next to Mom.

"Mom said, 'Dinah, your father and I have decided . . .' Et cetera. I already told you.

"The disaster freak in me must have been thirsty for

something much worse. Because, as I said, I didn't feel a thing.

"I remember I thought, Hey, it's stupid to worry about being dead. Nothing to it. You just don't feel anything, that's all.

"Then I thought, well, when you dive into really cold water, you don't feel anything either. The cold only hits you after a couple of seconds. When you burn yourself, you don't feel it either, not right away. One time I fell off my bike and scraped my knee raw. I still have a little scar there. But it took a while before it started to hurt.

"I gave it a couple of minutes, a couple of miles more of road. To pass the time I counted: Linda Dennis, Shawn McCarthy, Stacey Hines, Janie Vogelsang, all the kids I could think of who'd gone through the same thing. I wondered what *they* felt when they first heard.

"I gave it through three traffic lights, through the town of New Canaan. Still nothing. At least not about Mom and Dad. About myself, about this iciness in me, I started to feel bothered. Horrified. Other people would too, if they knew.

"While we were stopped for those lights, I tried to scare up normal feeling in myself, like when you scratch something that ought to itch. I went over my parents' recent fights in my mind: Mom turning off the TV in the middle of Dad's blueberry muffin commercial. Dad wisecracking about radiocarbon dating, as if he didn't know perfectly well it's a way archaeologists find out how old things are. Pretending it was a method for single people to meet and go out on dates. Mom reacting: Ha, ha, that was almost as funny as the gazpacho he spilled on his new Ralph Lauren tie.

" 'We won't squabble or be petty,' Mom explained to me. She and Dad would decide everything rationally. Like who'd keep what books, what furniture. 'We'll both stay friends with our good old friends, the Hammonds, the Morgans, the Grenells, the Steinfelds, not divide them up into his and hers like some ex-couples do. We'll stay civilized. We won't need lawyers, won't haul each other into court.' Mom said, after all, they were still the same people. They were not about to become each other's enemy. The last thing they wanted was to cause each other grief.

"I'd switched from reviewing their fights to totaling up their nights, twelve and a half years' worth—roughly four thousand five hundred—of lying in their double bed under the heirloom patchwork quilt Mom's grandma made from patches of Mom's childhood and teenage skirts, shorts, dresses, nightgowns, robes. I was wondering—none of my business!—how many times they'd, um, made love. Well, in a way, it *was* my business, since on one of those times they'd made me.

"Mom asked, 'Is there anything you'd like to ask?'

"Sure, one thing I was very curious about: Can you still call it love if, after you've made it, you don't love the other person anymore?

"Another thing: How would Mom feel if she knew that I, her child, was sitting there not feeling any emotion? Except by then I felt worried. What if I got a stepfather whom I couldn't stand? I already pictured his huge long loafers on our kitchen floor. That scene really stuck in my mind. I guess I thought the whole thing could be happening on account of it." I laugh. "I asked Mom, 'Are you going to marry somebody else?'

"Mom said, 'No.'

" 'Will Dad?'

" 'Not that I know of.'

"So then I asked why they were getting divorced.

"She said something about growing apart, their interests taking different directions."

I glance at Dr. Schneck. "Did you notice, so far in this session I've said *um* only once? I'm saying a lot more of the things I'm thinking."

She nods and motions to go on.

"The first time my mother ever saw my father—she used to love telling this story—was on the stage, in *A Midsummer Night's Dream*. Dad belonged to a theater company that came up to Ithaca, New York, when Mom was in her first year at Cornell. Mom had never seen a play by Shakespeare before. Dad played Theseus. No one could have played it more princely, wisely, or sexier, Mom always used to say. She must have thought he'd have a great stage career. But when he started getting more work for TV commercials, he did less and less acting. I asked if she felt bad about that. She denied it.

"I asked if Dad minded her getting so interested in archaeology, or that she was going on the dig. She said, No, he wanted her to.

"So then I asked a corny question, 'Did you guys just fall out of love?'

"Mom smiled—that I'd called them guys—I can still remember. Then she sucked in her lips, just for a moment. Her lips disappeared. Her face stopped being beautiful. It looked like it had a seam across it.

"Then she said, 'Your father and I will naturally both continue to love you as much as ever,' about as naturally as if she'd memorized this from a manual on how to tell your child about your divorce.

"I asked, 'Who gets me?' Just to say something, keep the conversation going. I naturally figured it would be the same arrangement as with other kids I knew.

"Mom said, 'I'm glad you asked. The answer is, *you'll* decide.'

" 'How do you mean?'

"Mom said something about my being grown-up enough and intelligent enough to sort out all the pluses and minuses for myself. I could take my time, no need to hurry. I could take till the end of camp, if I needed to. And she said, 'We won't try to influence you, or put any pressure on you, I promise.'

"I didn't see what was so hard about it. I'd already decided. Linda Dennis's father, Janie Vogelsang's father, too, had both moved down near the beach. It was starting to be a local custom for ex-husbands to live there, in ramshackle houses more like summer cottages that you could walk out the front door of, almost right onto the rocks and in the water. I said, 'I'll live with you half the year, and with Dad half the year. Doesn't that sound fair?'

" 'Yes, it sounds fair,' Mom said.

"The Datsun had bucket seats. I moved as far over toward Mom as I could. 'Okay if I turn on the radio?' The dial was still set on the station that had been playing oldies. Judy Collins sang 'Suzanne,' about a river, and boats going by. Well, we were coming into Rowayton, driving along the river there. I saw sailboats out my window, motorboats, yachts at anchor, covered with canvasses, masts poking into the sky. The sun was going down. *'And you want to travel with her,'* Judy Collins sang, then something about traveling blind; I don't know what it's supposed to mean. But the sun was sinking down below the line of trees across the river, and I looked out the car window straight at the sun, as you are not supposed to, and it blinded me. Well, not exactly blinded me, but I saw spots of light, turquoise, blue, green, aftersuns, in front of my eyes. This lasted a couple of minutes, and then we were home.

"The garage door was up, the Camaro was in there. Dad was home. He came out to greet us.

"They still had their language of looks—which I understood too. Dad's look said, Did you tell her? Mom's look said, Yes, and she took it okay.

"Dad said, 'Well, I found an apartment.'

"I thought that was lucky, because there were only one or two apartment buildings in the area.

" 'In a great neighborhood,' Dad said. 'Just a hop and a skip from a really top school.'

"I was in my last year of elementary school. There's only one junior high in Rowayton, and no one ever said of it that it was 'really tops.' Slowly, really slowly, this whole new idea dawned on me.

" 'Dad, you're moving away! Where are you moving to?'

" 'New York.' He gave Mom a look, How come you

129

left that out? 'Manhattan, right near Central Park, right near all kinds of great places; you're going to love it, I guarantee.'

"Mom said, 'I call that influencing her.'

"Dad said, 'Not at all. Whatever she decides, she'll spend *some* time with me there.'

"I thought, Wow, I'd been really blind, thinking nothing to it, half a year with him, half a year with her. That was out. I couldn't go to two schools.

"I went upstairs. I felt like being by myself.

"My room looked all wrong. Full of baby things I hadn't gotten around to putting away: beat-up old picture books still on my bookshelves. A dollhouse still under my window. A Barbie, a Raggedy Ann, and a decrepit stuffed elephant on my bed. I lunged out, swept the dolls off. The Barbie made a clunk, hitting the floor.

"My door squeaked open. I kicked it shut. I gave it such a wham, the whole house shook."

"But you did not feel anything?" Dr. Schneck asks evenly.

"Yes, I felt mad."

"At?"

"Myself. That it hadn't occurred to me that one of them might move away. I flopped down on my bed, on my stomach, with my boots on.

"I heard Dad come up the stairs.

"He knocked on my door. I didn't say come in. He came in anyway.

" 'Want me to help you off with those?'

"I didn't say yes.

"He started to pull on one boot.

"I sat up. He'd changed into his rumpled chino pants that he wore around the house and a faded blue work shirt. He gave me a boyish don't-blame-me grin.

" 'Mom said you went on a great trail ride.' Oh, that. It seemed so long ago, like from a previous incarnation. 'Well, I just thought I'd tell you, there's a good riding stable right in the heart of Manhattan, near where we, er, I, will live. There are bridle paths the length and breadth of Central Park.'

"I'd have the best room in the apartment, on weekends, or permanently, if I decided to move there. The school nearby was Hunter, the best in New York, people said. It had very hard entrance exams, in fact, coming up right around then, the following week. He bet I could pass.

"He 'propagandized' as hard as he could."

Dr. Schneck asks, "How did you feel about that?"

"I don't know. Okay, I guess. It *was* unfair, though. I minded, or, I figured, *should* mind, for Mom's sake. But I liked it too.

"Dad pulled at my other riding boot, huffing and groaning, to show it was a big effort. There, off at last. He collapsed onto the bed. He looked up at my pink-and-blue flowered wallpaper that he and Mom had picked out before I was born, and at my Sir Joshua Reynolds angel faces. He took my hand, stroked it.

"I said, 'You're the announcer in the family. How come *you* didn't tell me?'

"He said something boyish, like, 'I was too chicken,' in a please-still-like-me voice. He leaned on his elbow and looked in my eyes. 'You'll have just as good a life. I'll make it up to you, I promise. Come on, say you feel okay about it.'

"I said, 'Sure.' As okay as an iceberg floating in the Arctic Ocean. I think our bargain started then."

"What bargain?" asks Dr. Schneck.

"That he wouldn't have to discuss things with me like what went wrong between him and Mom. And I wouldn't have to tell him what I felt or did not feel.

"He sat the elephant on his chest. It was an old baby toy of his. He slung its trunk back and forth. He asked me not to be mad at him, or at Mom either.

"I remember, I told myself not to look at him then. But I couldn't help it, I did—just like in the dream! He still had this dopey don't-be-mad grin on. But his eyes were wet. So I looked away. Or I would have seen him cry. You know what? I feel good, I feel relieved!"

"Yes? About the dream?"

"Right, it makes it not about Gray, less like I did a bad thing to *him*. I don't know; I just feel better. I guess I really needed this extra time to spill my guts out. Thank you!"

She sits forward, holds her delicate, pale, wrinkled finger to her chin and says, "You felt very strongly that you wanted this extra session, isn't that so?"

"Yes."

"During it you 'spilled' your 'guts out'—about *not* feeling things." She smiles. "Does that sound like a contradiction?"

I smile back. A kind of excitement is starting in me. "Yes, but it really isn't."

"Oh?" She leans forward, curious. "How do you mean?"

"Well, because—I started to figure this out before, as I was talking—feeling nothing *is* a feeling. *That* sounds like a contradiction too."

She nods; she knows it's not.

"Like, when Mom gave me her little speech, promising they'd naturally continue to love me. How could she say that to me? Look what happened to the promise they'd made each other, the promise all married people make, to love each other for always! I was thinking, What happened to *that*? But thinking *is* feeling. At least when you're fighting your feelings with everything you've got."

I can see in her face that she has followed me, every step, this far. She asks, "Why did you have to fight them?"

Isn't it obvious? "So as not to make things worse."

"Worse, how?"

"I don't know. I can't explain. It's like I've come to a roadblock."

She sits back. "Try just saying what comes to your mind."

"Mount Ashcroft. My mad climb up the steep path. Mad is right! That time I *did* make things worse." The image assails me of my father in my bunk sitting on my bed, head in his hands.

"Mad at whom?"

"Myself!"

"What for?"

"Look, please don't think I thought this then. Although it seems so obvious now, I don't understand how I could ever *not* have known: Mom's not coming proved my point: Promises were worthless. Even simple promises, like to show up on Parents' Weekend. The only way it could be all right, the only way it could *not* mean Mom had stopped caring about me, was if she was dead. So that's what I must have wished—wished hard enough to believe. Which is about as mad as a person can be. Not just at myself. At *her* too.

"The mind's weird. At least mine is. All these years, I didn't know this. Presumably, because I couldn't bear to know it, wouldn't have liked myself if I'd known. But now that I *do* know, I'm glad. I mean, I'd rather have had emotions, even awful ones, even"—say it!— "murderous ones, than no emotions at all. And just think"—I lean forward, I say to her face—"I might not have figured all these things out, if you hadn't offered me this extra session."

She says, "What do you think about this: You wanted very much to come for this extra session. Yet the suggestion had to come from me."

"I don't think anything of it! *I* couldn't have asked for it, could I?"

She looks at me in such a kind and pleasant, reasonable way—oh, I'm going to miss coming here and seeing her!—and she asks me very seriously, "Why not?"

"Well, because people just don't."

Her eyebrow moves an infinitesimal distance up.

People don't? Who cares? I'm not "people." Is the question justified? Why *couldn't* I have asked?

As the session ends I'm thinking about other things:

I'll stop at D'Agostino's on my way to Jonathan's; I'll buy stuff to make chili, he's always asking me to. Gray'll come over and have it with us. Afterward the three of us can go to a movie. And later, after Jonathan's asleep, the two of us . . . All the while, the answer's coming closer. By the time I'm out the door, I almost, almost, know.

XII

Monday, May 9, 3:40–4:30 P.M.

"Gray gave me this, do you like it?" I slip it off my wrist, show it to Dr. Schneck: A slender silver bracelet with a raised spine down the middle and twelve roses, engraved to perfection, with veins in the tiny rose leaves and infinitesimal thorns on the stems.

She says, "It's beautiful."

I put it back on. "He was going to wait till just before he goes home for the summer." Only ten more days! My breath sticks in my throat. I think of the long months ahead of being apart. I bend the bracelet tighter. It's open-ended, that's its style. I worry about losing it. I don't have a present for him yet. Too bad I.D. bracelets are corny. The idea of something with a good strong clasp appeals to me a lot.

"He gave it to me last night, while we were waiting for my aunt and uncle to come back. Jonathan said he had such a great time he wanted them to go away for another weekend, so I'd come and take care of him again.

"We took him to the aquarium. Gray let him stand on the platform inside the fence and toss mackerel and herrings to the belugas. Belinda swam right up and let him pop one in her mouth. Jonathan was thrilled, and told us he'll definitely be a cetologist when he grows up.

"I took my Milton final this morning. My favorite passage showed up as one of the essay choices. Where Adam says to God, 'Among unequals what society/Can sort what harmony or true delight?' Meaning, the animals weren't the right company; he was lonely and asked God to create him a mate. And God answered—I love the way He put it—'A nice and subtle happiness I see/ Thou to thyself proposest. . . .' I wrote about the fine time Adam and Eve started out to have. I threw in some lines I know by heart, that Professor Halloran likes; he always quotes them. They're from the nuptial bower passage, starting with 'Disporting, till the amourous Bird of Night/ Sung spousal. . . .' I bet he gives me an A. Not that it matters. I shouldn't care that much about grades anymore.

"It's funny; I was kind of hoping to see the girl who chews on her hair in the elevator today."

"Why?"

"I don't know; she was just on my mind, I guess. I've thought a lot about what you said about the extra session. I really wanted it. And it's true; you had to ask me. One thing about that really bothers me."

"Yes? What bothers you?"

"Do you figure I was that way with my mother?"

"How do you mean?"

Come on, *you* know! Don't make me say it. I squirm in my chair. I take a handful of hair—hey, I nearly stuck it in my mouth! I flick it over my shoulder, as if that's what I meant to do with it. "I don't *know* how I mean. I go around in circles trying to figure it out.

"I still say my parents were right to let me decide. I mean, I wasn't the marble-top coffee table, just one of the inanimate objects; I had a mind of my own. Sorry I'm raising my voice. It's just this is so important to me!"

"It's all right to raise your voice. Yes, it is important." She leans forward. "To go back for just a moment, does anything more occur to you about the girl in the elevator who chews on her hair?"

"Just something really obvious. She reminds me of me. I used to do that. I did it on my jewelweed morning."

"Can you tell me about that?"

"It was my first morning home from camp. My deadline for telling my decision.

"Dad had wanted me to tell it right away, the day before, when they picked me up at Adventurers' Inn. That was the rendezvous place, where the camp buses left us off and our parents picked us up. It's just across the Whitestone Bridge, in Queens. But Mom said, 'She's

138

tired. Let's wait till tomorrow, after she's had a good night's sleep.' Which I did not have.

"Every little noise woke me up: cars on the road, neighborhood dogs barking, creaks the house made. It got more exhausting trying to go back to sleep every time than just staying awake. I got up around dawn. I had hours to kill before my parents would wake up. They were in separate rooms, Mom upstairs, Dad in the family room.

"I tried to read, went for a long bike ride. I climbed up to my tree house. Up there I went over everything again in my mind for the sevenhundredumpteenth time; at least I went over the pluses:

"Number One: Hunter, a terrific school, from seventh grade all the way through twelfth. Over three thousand kids took the entrance tests. Only three hundred fifty got in, and I was one of them. You know something? I'm still proud of that, after all these years.

"Dad had driven me in the day of the tests. After they were over, we'd gone on a tour of the school. It looks kind of like a fortress or a prison from the outside. But the inside looked great to me, good-size classrooms, up-to-date labs, more books in the library than in a few Fairfield County, Connecticut, junior high schools and high schools put together. Being reasonably brainy at Hunter would be fine, I could tell, unlike in Rowayton, where, if you let it show, especially in junior high, it makes you a pariah.

"Plus Number Two: The apartment was great. Dad was still fixing it up. In the spring, before the furniture came, spending weekends there had been fun, like camping out.

"Plus Number Three: all of New York. He moved there in February. I spent a lot of weekends with him between then and July, when I went to camp. And we did a lot of exploring. We went to Chinatown, SoHo, the Empire State Building, we walked across the Brooklyn Bridge, saw all the terrific places."

"What about the pluses in Rowayton?" asks Dr. Schneck.

"I'd had those all my life. I didn't have to go over them."

"Let me put it this way: What about the pluses, and the minuses, of staying with your mother? Did you go over those when you were up in your tree house?"

"I don't think so." I feel kind of sick to my stomach. "I don't know. Maybe that was unfair of me."

"Tell me, what was it like, for you with your mother during those months, after your father moved out?"

I take a deep breath, sit back, breathe it out. "That'll be hard to describe."

"Try."

"It was special. Heightened. You know what I mean?"

"Not quite. Not yet. But you will tell me."

"Well, for instance, I tried to notice things more. Like, things starting to come up outside. In case— This is hard to say."

"Say it anyway."

"In case it was my last spring to notice things like that: little green shoots. White-tipped snowdrop buds. Even the smelly skunk cabbage along the brook. Fiddlehead ferns, growing from coiled tight to fully unfurled. The spotted leaves of dogtooth violets all through our woods, that I'd always just thought of as weeds.

"In a way it was like that in school. Kids in my class seemed more special. Ellen Steinfeld and I got even closer, maybe because now something dramatic was happening in *my* life too.

"And Ricky Sturges, my longtime crush, started noticing me. Pretty soon he and I were 'going together.' All we did was touch a little, kiss a little, 'hang out,' and I learned to shoot baskets. Oh, but it was happiness! Because I had all the right feelings. When we were together, I could stop worrying about being an iceberg. In fact, I had to try not to let it show too much how thrilled I was by it all. And even after we broke up, it was still thrilling. I indulged in bittersweet nostalgia of looking back on lost romance. It was so comforting to feel all the feelings you're supposed to feel, including healthy loathing for Tracy Williams, whom he went with after me. It sounds so juvenile! But I felt older than my age, and as though I were growing up fast.

"Mom treated me accordingly. She finally stopped getting me sitters, except when I needed rides and she couldn't drive me herself. She respected my privacy more. Stopped doing surprise room checks to see how many pieces of clothing were lying on my floor. Didn't remind me to wash the back of my neck. In return I was supposed to respect her privacy. It was like a testing period."

"How?"

"Well, I had to live up to their—her—belief in me.

You know. That I had good judgment, could make up my mind on my own.

"And not bug her. Like not ask, Mom, when was the last time you had a Rocky Road ice cream cone? I was supposed not to notice things like she never went to Baskin-Robbins anymore. She used to go almost every day. We'd kidded about how far she'd travel for that flavor. One time the Baskin-Robbins in Rowayton was out of it, so she'd driven right on up to the one in Norwalk. That sounds like a small thing. But she stopped liking other foods, lost weight, got skinny without trying, and gave up on other things, too, dropped out of her tennis game with the same group of women she'd played with for years. Stopped having people over for meals and drinks. Only the Steinfelds, once in a while.

"They were the only ones she stayed friends with. The others called and invited her to things, but she wouldn't go. I overheard her saying to the Steinfelds that the others really all preferred Dad and were only being nice.

"She had her friends at school. At least I hoped so. I even almost started to hope, though I dreaded it too, that she was seeing Professor Levinson, if that would make her happy. I prepared myself for coming home and finding him there one of those days. But it didn't happen.

"She was very caught up in schoolwork. She spent hours studying for her comprehensives and writing her senior paper. She got highest honors. I was at her graduation, and very proud of her.

"We had these archaeological conversations. She'd tell

me things like that an implement had been dug up from twenty-five thousand years ago that people had ground up corn with, or showed me photos of serrated cutting tools from even longer ago. I couldn't see the serrated edges. They looked like plain old slabs of stone. But I'd act interested, to keep her going. At least when she talked about that stuff she had some of her sparkle and liveliness back.

"Don't get the wrong idea. We had nice times too. We did things together, went to the beach, out to dinner, to the movies. Like two grown-up friends almost. I tried to be good company. Sometimes I even prepared lists in my head of cheerful topics to bring up; I carefully avoided any subjects that might make her uncomfortable. Like, things I'd done with Dad over the weekend. Especially if Dad's then friend, Valerie, had been there, and especially if we'd had fun. One time, at the Good Earth, a Chinese restaurant we liked, I really blew it. The fortune set me up: 'Reveal your heart's desire!' Mom said, 'Go ahead.' And I blurted, 'Oh, Mom, I just wish you were your old self!'

"She looked as if I'd kicked her. 'Thanks a lot; I really needed that.'

Dr. Schneck looks at me so kindly, I feel ashamed. "I'm telling this wrong; it really wasn't all so grim. It was a special time, really. A time of—I already told you. I can't define it. Of expecting something. I woke up every morning with a sense of, Today it'll happen. . . ."

Dr. Schneck is all attention. "Can you tell me more?"

"No. I can conjure back the feel of it; I just can't fit words around it."

"Try to say what's going through your mind."

"It was *just the opposite* of standing under my tree house, massacring the jewelweed pods. I know that doesn't make sense. I'll tell you something great, that I *didn't* expect, though, that Mom did, okay?"

Open-hands gesture.

"On the last day of school she and I and Ellen and Mr. and Mrs. Steinfeld were going to have supper at the beach. Then Mom said she had to pick something up in town first and might be delayed, so she wanted me to go with the Steinfelds; we'd meet by the picnic tables. Fine, I didn't think anything of it.

"When we got down to the beach, as soon as I got out of the car, I smelled a lot more smoke than from the one grill the five of us would have used. Odors of corn roasting and seafood baking wafted my way. Four picnic tables had been pushed together to make one big one, set with party stuff. Twelve of my friends—I'll never know how Mom kept them from spilling the beans—came racing at me, yelling *Surprise!*

"Mom had secretly planned this for weeks, hired people to help with the food, even hired a rock group, consisting of Ricky's older brother Doug on guitar and two ninth-graders on drums and bass. And there was a huge cake, not from the crummy bakery in town, but from the good one all the way in Greenwich, with HAPPY GRADUATION spelled out across the top.

"After everybody started eating, there was still one empty place. I didn't think anything of it. A car door slammed in the parking lot. It could have been anybody.

"Well, it was Dad!

"I ran to him. By then the group was playing. He swooped me up. Nobody was dancing yet. That didn't bother him; he danced with me over to the party. He's a natural, even when he doesn't know the step. He can follow any beat, even no beat, so we didn't look too foolish.

"When it was time to cut the cake, he and Mom stood there with me. I made a real mess of the first few slices, dropped crumbs all over the place." The specialness rushes back. Standing in the middle of all the noise and laughing, the cake knife in my hands, thinking, These are my friends; I've known most of them since nursery school. This is the beach I was a baby at and have always come to; this is the kind of party I've longed to have. . . . I try to explain this to Dr. Schneck. I thought, And now my whole life might change; by next year these might not be my friends anymore. . . . I try to convey to Dr. Schneck how—oddly, weirdly—the idea of my moving away, which was, after all, a good fifty percent probability by then, absolutely refused to become real in my mind.

She thinks about it, finger to her chin. She says, "Could your feeling of expecting something have had to do with hoping that your parents might get back together?"

I sigh. I give her a condescending smile. I think, all those degrees and certificates on her wall attesting to her expertise on the human psyche, and this is what she comes up with!

"Of course." I sound like I'm talking to someone

slightly retarded. "That's what *all* kids of parents splitting up hope, openly or secretly." Who doesn't know that? "No. It had nothing to do with my feeling of expecting something. Sorry, I don't mean to sound so snide."

She looks at me sadly. The sadness matches how I feel. "You did not sound so snide. You sounded—" Hold it; I know the word she'll use. "You sounded disappointed, in me. I think you hoped that I would know exactly what you expected."

Yes, it's true. I still am. I can still taste it in my mouth; it's not just my hair, it's the taste of disappointment, standing there, bursting the pods, and the time was running out.

XIII

Thursday, May 12, 4:20–5:10 P.M.

"When I left here Monday, I shoved all that stuff out of my mind so I could enjoy the walk home. I looked in store windows on the way. Then I saw this great, stunning belt in a men's shop on Third Avenue, and I thought: just right for Gray.

"I went in, asked what it costs. Eleven hundred dollars! The salesman told me the price in a bored, preppie tone, as though he knew lots of people who wouldn't think twice, spending that kind of money. The ornaments were sterling silver, he explained to me snottily; the turquoises were genuine; it was all 'hand-wrought' by Navaho craftsmen.

"I had to laugh: an eleven-hundred dollar belt holding up Gray's seven-dollar thrift-shop jeans! And I wondered what the Navaho craftsman who'd hand-wrought it got paid. A pittance, probably.

"Then I passed by Plant World, you know that store? The droopy petunias and parched-looking other plants made me think of how our place had looked when I got home from camp. I guess seeing the belt had already started me thinking of that day.

"It was sad, coming home. The garden looked awful. The lawn had burned-out patches. Nothing was in bloom, no begonias or geraniums around the terrace. Mom said she'd put some out. Those were practically her first words, after 'Hello, you look great,' when she first saw me. Oh, and telling me I should sit in front, next to Dad. She'd sat in the back.

"I remember thinking, for the first time in my whole childhood, when I first caught sight of Mom out the camp bus window that day: She doesn't look great. Tanned, yes, but her skirt hung too loose, she'd gotten really skinny. And her hair didn't fluff out, was cut too short. Unevenly, too. Whoever had done it wasn't much of a hair cutter.

"Anyhow, I rushed upstairs to see the presents she'd brought. Guess what, an Indian belt. Way too big on me. It flopped around my hips. Anyway, back then, nobody wore belts like that. The other present—after all the trouble I'd taken, acting so grown-up all those months—was a doll. Wow. I'll tell you about that later.

"Monday, when I got home from here, I called her up and asked what happened to the belt.

"She said it was right in her closet.

"Great, could I come take a look at it? How about the next day, Tuesday? I had my Anthropology final in the afternoon, but nothing in the morning.

"Mom had student conferences scheduled all Tuesday morning. How about Friday? She'd be free then.

"Friday I have my Art History final. Besides, I didn't want to wait.

"Mom said, Okay, I could come tomorrow. She was just sorry she wouldn't be there. She'd leave the key in the usual place. The belt would be on my bed.

"Dad lent me the car. I got there around ten, went straight upstairs. I liked the belt even better than the one in the store. It's lighter and narrower, more graceful-looking. She must have polished up the silver ornaments. It has three oval, shell-shaped ones and four smaller, squash-blossom shaped ones, all with turquoises in the center. It has a neat silver clasp, good and strong.

"I put it on. It was about five inches too wide around my waist. So I knew it would fit Gray. Okay, terrific, mission accomplished. I'd found what I'd come for: an incredibly valuable present that I could give him without spending a dime. Somehow, though—I don't know why—all the excitement drained out of the idea.

"I thought, What if Gray saw that other belt, or one like it, in a store and felt embarrassed, overwhelmed, by the amount of money such belts sell for nowadays? True, that could happen. But it didn't explain why I kept on standing there with the belt around my hips, instead of putting it in my bag and leaving.

"It was weird standing in front of the mirror over my

old bureau in my old childhood room. Like playing hooky from my regular life. And I had this premonition that any second I would start feeling really, really low.

"I tried to fend it off. I lay down on my bed and tried to 'listen' to my thoughts—like I'm supposed to do here, in this room. Do you know what I mean?"

She nods.

"I'm so used to the din and roar of New York, I'd forgotten how quiet our house is. It had rained pretty hard while I was driving. Now it was letting up. Isolated drops fell on the roof. Some crows cawed from down near the road. And the house made creaks. Like on that night home from camp. I thought, it wasn't so much the noises I'd heard that had kept waking me up. It was something I had *waited* to hear, had *not* heard—footsteps, coming toward my room.

"I got up, decided to look for the doll. I rummaged through boxes of my old things in the back of my closet. Not there. I went into Mom's room. It's more like an office than a bedroom with her desk and bookcases and the glassed-in cabinet that had stood in the family room.

"In there was the doll, right on the middle shelf, between animal figures and pottery shards.

"I took it out. It's a kachina doll. Do you know what those are?"

"Hopi Indian dolls. I don't know anything about them."

"They have to do with Hopi religion. This doll Mom brought me is wooden. It's about five inches tall. It has a blue face, round blue wooden knobs for ears sticking out of the sides of its head, painted crescent-shape eyes, no nose, a mouth with painted zig-zaggy teeth, no neck, a painted-on shirt, a lampshade-shaped skirt, little red moccasins, and it's holding a little shovel. Oh, and it's got wispy hair.

"I thought, Ugh, bad enough she thought I still played with dolls, did it have to be so ugly? 'How old is it?' I'd asked politely.

"It wasn't even old. She'd gotten somebody to make it.

"Well, Tuesday I was thinking about my Anthropology final coming up. We haven't studied the Hopis as such, but a question could turn up about totems, animism, something like that. I took down a book of Mom's, read around.

"Kachinas are spirits. They grant fertility, make the corn grow, send rain. They go away for half the year. At ceremonial dances the Hopis dress up like them. And if they get everything exactly right, the costumes, masks, headgear, dance routines—Mom already told me some of this stuff when she was studying it—a magic happens whereby they actually *become* the kachinas, for as long as the dance lasts.

"Same with the dolls. They give them to girl children, and magic's supposed to happen."

"What magic?"

"Oh, like having your cake and eating it too. When the kachinas are away, the little girls still have the dolls, and that's supposed to be just as good. It's primitive. Pathetic. Besides, the book was written in textbookese. I fell asleep over it.

151

"When I woke up, the first thing I saw on the pillow next to me was the blue-faced figure with the knob ears, painted eyes, wispy hair, and I didn't know what time it was or where I was. Oh, right . . . in Mom's room, this was her bed. And it was late, I had to get moving.

"I put things back, straightened the bed, went downstairs.

"I was putting the house key back in the usual place, up on the lintel above the front door, when Mom's car turned into the driveway. She called out her window, 'I'm glad you're still here,' and pulled up next to the Volvo.

"She'd been able to shift around some appointments. She'd called to tell me, but I hadn't arrived yet.

"We had our usual unrelaxed hello. I held the keys to the Volvo in my hand. Mom said, 'Good thing I drove fast.' And she asked . . ." Here my voice gives me trouble. Levolors, help me out, hold my gaze! Because if I look at Dr. Schneck now, I doubt I'll get this said.

Dr. Schneck asks, "What did your mother ask?"

"She asked me, 'Can you stay awhile?' That was it! What I'd waited for. Without knowing! How could I not have known, right along? The whole night long, I waited for her to come in my room and ask me, Dinah, stay! And out in the woods, when I did the jewelweed pods, I was waiting. It was just a short walk from the house; she could still have come! Even after she called me to breakfast, there could still have been time, if Dad was still asleep.

"He was up, frying eggs. 'Well, Dinah, who's it going to be?' he asked all bright and cheerfully.

"The refrigerator door was open. Mom crouched on her heels, looking for something in there. I sat down to breakfast, the opposite of hungry.

"Dad flipped two eggs—'Ta-da! yolks intact'—onto my plate. They stared at me like bulging eyes. I got queasy.

" 'Well, Dinah?'

"Mom was still crouched behind the Coldspot door, I couldn't see her face. 'You, Dad.'

"I don't know if she even heard. She said, 'There. It was hiding behind the Crisco can.' The raspberry jam! She brought it to the table. She asked, Did I want any?

"Anyway, on Tuesday, in the driveway, I said, 'Sure, I can stay awhile.'

"We went inside. Mom to the kitchen, I to the phone. I called up school. You have to let the health service know if you're going to miss a final.

"She improvised a lunch with her usual perfection: cottage cheese and fruit, house-and-gardenishly surrounded by olives, watercress, red pepper rings, and glasses of iced tea with lemon wedges and fresh mint sprigs.

"The weather had cleared; the sun was shining into the kitchen. Out the windows the azaleas were in their glory. Rosy-breasted house finches, sparrows, and chickadees took their turns at the feeder.

"Mom asked what made me think of the belt.

"I told her about seeing the one in the store.

"She said, 'Yes, those belts are in style. I've thought of asking if you wanted to get it made smaller, but I wasn't sure you'd—' She changed the subject to small talk about Wesleyan, her students, finals.

" 'Mom, I'm missing my Anthropology final.'

" 'Why? When is it?' She got concerned.

" 'In half an hour. Don't worry; I'll get it deferred. I'll take it in September. Before I leave for Florida. The reason is, I wanted to stay awhile. Because you asked me to.'

" 'Good, I'm glad.' But she sounded nervous.

" 'Mom, I want to ask you some things.'

" 'Go ahead.' She looked out the window at the feeder.

" 'That summer when you were in Arizona. How was it for you?'

" 'I loved it. I threw myself into it as hard as I could.'

" 'How was it, coming back?'

" 'Not so good. Could we *not* talk about that?' She concentrated on the birds as if they needed her gaze to keep their traffic orderly.

" 'I want to, Mom. I need to.' I didn't know what I was going to say next. I hadn't planned this."

Dr. Schneck asks, "What did you say next?"

" 'Mom, all the kids I knew with parents splitting up stayed with their mothers!'

" 'Dinah, we went over it at the time; you agreed, it was fairer—'

"I burst out, 'Mom, didn't you realize how I felt?' I was being unfair. I was springing stuff on her I had only just realized myself. I couldn't stop myself, though. 'You *made* me choose Dad! You didn't want me!'

"She sucked her lips in. She got that seam-across-the-face look.

154

" 'Talk to me, Mom. Tell me how it felt to you.'

"She said, 'Like in a shipwreck. Like everything had failed. Like I'd failed everything.' I don't remember how she put it, exactly. She sounded matter-of-fact. She said, 'I tried not to let it show. That would have been very unfair to you.'

" 'It showed, Mom.' I felt good saying this, like I had the right to, like I was clearing the air. Hindsight is cheap though. Cheaper than Airwick, or Lysol spray. 'You must have been really depressed, Mom.'

" 'Be that as it may,' Mom said professorially, 'in my then frame of mind, I thought it best not to inflict myself on you too much. I thought you needed—deserved —a cheerful atmosphere.'

" 'You see! I was right! Whatever the reason, you didn't want me around. I didn't have a free choice! It was rigged! There was no way I could have chosen right!' I felt pleased with myself. I couldn't wait to tell *you*. I thought you'd be pleased that I finally saw this clearly. I wallowed in hindsight and self-pity. Till my on-top-of-things professorial mom let her head drop down on her linen place mat. Her pretty, fluffy hair got in the cottage cheese. Her shoulders shook.

"I went over, touched her gingerly on the back. She said, with her head in that position, 'Dinah, it can't help but be rough when a marriage breaks up. I did my best to keep some of that off your shoulders.'

" 'You made it rougher on me in some ways than it had to be,' I couldn't keep from saying.

" 'Please, Dinah.' She didn't lift her head up.

"I thought, You still don't really want me around! At least I refrained from saying it aloud. But I couldn't sit there any longer waiting for her to look at me. I left the table, went upstairs.

"I went into her room. I stood in front of the glassed-in cabinet, looking at the ugly doll with the wisps of hair glued on. The kachina dolls—there were lots of photographs in the book I'd looked at—all had either no hair, or black hair painted on. Why was this one's hair so light? I thought about this with a part of my mind, while the rest of me was mad, ashamed, and I don't know what all else.

"I heard her footsteps come up the stairs. She came into the room. She came right up behind where I stood. Her soft hair touched my cheek. We're almost the same height. I turned around to her. Our faces touched. I'd been crying. Mom, too. Our cheeks were touching, so my tears and Mom's ran down both our cheeks together, and we didn't know which tears were whose.

"Then I had to kind of smile, right in the middle of crying. Because, how come I'd been so blind? It was suddenly so clear: I held up the kachina doll, compared her hair to Mom's—same! Of course. I remembered Mom's looking so ragged when she came home from Arizona. She'd cut it herself, and had given snips of it to the carver, to stick onto the doll's head. To make the doll more of a stand-in for her. For me to keep near me always. And I didn't even want it! How did that make her feel? Do you understand this?"

Dr. Schneck nods.

"I held the doll and Mom held me, and we stood like

that a good minute or two, swaying back and forth a little, and it wasn't exactly magic, but we were pretty close.

"Phew, I didn't think I'd get all of this said. I feel emptied out." I look around this room, imagine it without me sitting in this chair. Only two more sessions! Only one more minute left of this one. I talk into the blue, fast:

"The big, raw deal when your parents split up is, it lets in the idea that love stops. Not just the idea, the reality. Because one of them stops loving the other. Or both do. Right in front of you! And no matter how often they say it won't happen, can't happen, it can: They *can* stop loving you! Or vice versa, you them. Which is worse? I don't know. Anybody whom you love can stop loving you. And vice versa. Next to dying, that's the scariest thing there can be. I guess it's less scary to assume you don't love them in the first place. Okay, you don't love them. So then if they stop loving you, okay too, it's not as bad. Is what I'm saying old hat? Is is just a cliché? Am I the only one who hasn't known this right along?"

Dr. Schneck says, "Let's go back a little. Earlier, when you realized what it was you expected of your mother, you expressed surprise that you hadn't known right along. That's because insight is a *re*cognition. That explains why it's accompanied by the feeling, How could I ever not have known?

"Here's what I think about clichés. They start as truths. They only become clichés by being repeated often, thoughtlessly. What you said just now, concerning

157

love, you said for the first time. You said it thoughtfully. Yes, love can stop. No, that is not a cliché. It is a truth, hard to accept. To deny it, to shut it out by assuming it is you who do not feel, do not love, is even harder, and more costly. I think you think so too."

The minute's up. She goes on. "Some people keep on loving. Is that not also true?"

I give a huge sigh. "I'd give up everything—everything!—to be someone who can."

She smiles. "Doesn't that sound a bit drastic?" She stands. "See you Monday. Perhaps we can talk more about it then."

XIV

Monday, May 16, 3:40–4:30 P.M.

"I love your new hairdo." Instead of swept straight back, she wears it parted on the side. It comes forward over her ears. I can only see the earlobes this way. They have tiny pearls in them. "But I miss seeing the rest of your ears."

She smiles. "I can still hear you just as well."

"Do you notice anything different about me?"

"You are wearing the belt. It's very beautiful."

"Yes. I got this whole other idea for what to give Gray." I unfasten the clasp, hand her the belt.

She passes it through her hands, admires each ornament. "Thank you for letting me see it." She hands it back.

I put it on again. "I guess I'll start with the biggest event. The one that made the news. It's a girl!"

"The baby whale?" she asks.

"Right. She's five foot four, weights one hundred thirty-seven pounds, and she's the most beautiful creature, so they named her Beauty. She was born on Friday morning, at twenty after seven.

"I had to go take my Art History final. Afterward I took the subway down to the aquarium.

"The main exhibit hall was closed. I had to ask to have Gray paged. They were keeping people out, to give the whales the quiet they needed.

"Gray came out looking like some creature from the deep, in his black rubber wet suit, with his diving mask still dangling down his back. It was a first for me, hugging somebody dressed like that.

"In the ocean, if the mother whale's too tired, other females in the herd carry the newborn up to the surface, to start it breathing. In captivity, if the mother won't, people have to do it. If not, the calf can die. One did a few years ago, in another aquarium. That was one reason they've been keeping a twenty-four-hour watch. At first Gray and Phil, together, hoisted Beauty up three times so she could breathe. Then Belinda took over. Pretty soon Beauty started doing it on her own.

"She's iridescent oyster-white. She came swimming right up to the glass. She flattened out her melon. That's the round, rubbery-looking bulge on belugas' foreheads. It has something to do with how they pick up

160

sonar waves. Hers is still too big on her; she'll have to grow into it. She sent up bubbles through her blow hole; I think she was burping. And when she looked at me—she has the clearest, sky-blue eyes—I couldn't help thinking, new as she is, she already knows things that humans can only imagine."

"What things?"

"Well, like, that the beluga pool at the New York Aquarium is a far cry from, say, the Antarctic, but that being alive, swimming around with Belinda, is a pretty good deal anyway.

"Gray'd done something heroic. He would never have told me himself. I overheard the director telling it to visitors, two cetologists from the Museum of Natural History and the head of the New England Aquarium, who'd flown down to see Beauty.

"Belinda'd started giving birth, when the male, Alabaster, acted up. He's enormous, eighteen feet, and weighs almost two thousand pounds. He flailed around. He whopped the water with his tail, snapped his jaws ferociously, as if he had more of an appetite for a big breakfast than for becoming a father. They're not known to attack their young in the wild. But you can't predict how they'll behave in a pool. And no one had thought to drop the divider down. Well, Gray decided this was the moment. But the thing was stuck. So in he went, even though Big Al was clearly in no mood for visitors, and he managed to free the mechanism from below, fast. The divider came down, with a big loud clunk, just in the nick of time.

"The visitors were impressed. Gray was embarrassed.

I got so scared, retroactively, I grabbed him, in front of all those people.

"Meantime Beauty had propelled herself right to the sweet spot, which was smart of her, because whales' mammary glands are hidden inside folds, and was nursing away. 'Atta girl,' Gray said.

"He changed into regular clothes. We had frankfurters and orange drinks at the aquarium cafeteria overlooking the beach. I wanted to go down there. But he'd been up the whole night; he said all he wanted to do was sit on a bench on the boardwalk and watch the waves roll in.

"He stretched out his legs, put his head in my lap. I traced his eyebrows with my finger, smoothed down the straggly hairs. He pulled my head down, kissed me. He said, 'This is the greatest day of my life,' closed his eyes, and was out like a light.

"So then I watched the ocean by myself. I thought of herds of belugas, and other kinds of whales, swimming free, farther north, of someday going up there with Gray, watching them come up to play, spout fountains through their blow holes, mate—that would be a thrilling sight—and bring their babies up to breathe.

" 'Hey, you two loveboids,' called Carmine. He's one of the patrollers. He came over to get us.

"Gray jumped up. 'What happened? Is Beauty okay?'

" 'Fine and dandy. Someone's asking for you is all.'

"We went back. I said, 'Who do you wish it would be?'

" 'Mackleson,' Gray said. 'Then he could see her for himself, and I wouldn't have to write the final section of my project. Better still, Dr. Dobrosh, offering me a teaching fellowship on a silver platter, anytime I want.' Dobrosh is the head of the biology department. 'Hell, as long as I'm wishing, make it my old man.' Gray went into a whole quick fantasy about his father hearing the news on TV, flying right on up to say, 'I've seen the light, son. I'll let you off your promise, I reckon Dawson Construction can do without you this summer. You stay and keep an eye on that little whale, Beauty, and your other beauty, too.' Gray squeezed my hand, speaking for his father with an extra-thick Florida drawl.

"I said, 'Yeah, wouldn't that be great?' But I spun my own fantasy about who I wished it would be; pretty childish, but what was the harm? And you know what?"

"No, but you will tell me."

"It was Mom! Running to the gate where she was waiting, I thought about what you said last time. It's true she'd made it hard for me, I don't take any of that back. Even so, she's one of those people. She'd kept on . . . in her own way . . . the only way she could manage. . . ."

"Kept on doing what? You can say it," Dr. Schneck urged me in the same tone of voice I use to tell kids teetering on the edge of the diving board, Go ahead, you can do it. "Let yourself."

Ready, set: "Mom *did* keep on loving me." I laugh. "Though of course she'd come there to see Beauty. It was her day off from Wesleyan. She said, 'Gray, I hope you don't think it's presumptuous of me, taking advantage of knowing you personally. I would just love to have a look at that whale while she's still new, if you can arrange it.'

"Gray said with his most winning smile, 'It'll be my pleasure.'

"The three of us went in. Mom and I stayed just a short while, till Gray's next shift began.

"We went to the parking lot. She'd drive me home, on her way back to Connecticut. When we came to her car, she said, 'Wait, don't get in yet.' She reached into the glove compartment. 'Here. See if this fits you now.' The belt; she'd had it made smaller.

" 'Oh, Mom!' I put it on. It fit me perfectly. I was so happy! It would have been a big mistake, giving it to Gray. I mean, it just means so much more to me. Anyway, Mom and I hugged for a pretty long time, and the longer we hugged, the less nervous we got with each other.

"I've worn it every day. It goes with everything. Oh, and I've thought of what to give Gray. I'll tell you about that later.

"On the ride home Mom sprang this whole new thing on me. It's intriguing. But I don't know what to do."

"Tell me about it."

"Remember, I mentioned a Professor McVeigh, he was at Mom's, on Easter? Well, he's heading an archaeological survey out in North Dakota this summer. A gas company wants to run a pipeline through there. The purpose of the survey is to identify potential archaeological dig sites, so the gas company can take measures to protect them. He's hiring staff right now. Mom will be one of the supervisors. She said living conditions would be primitive, tents, privies, no running water, but it's beautiful country, and it could turn up some interesting finds.

"The crew will be mostly archaeology and geology majors, but that's not a requirement. The pay's pretty good. It starts June tenth. You don't have to sign on for the whole summer. The minimum stint is three weeks. There'll be five crews, so I could be in somebody else's. Mom wouldn't have to be my boss.

"We were driving along the Gowanus Canal. A huge freighter went by. Farther out I could see an ocean liner. I thought of the January sun setting behind the sail-boats and yachts at anchor in the Rowayton River. And here I had this opportunity to say, Yeah, Mom, I'll go, I'll travel with you."

I sit forward in my chair. I say to Dr. Schneck, "You probably think I should have."

She asks me, "Why do you think that?"

"Oh, because of everything I've been talking about. Because going out there with Mom this summer would make a nice, neat ending."

"Ending to what?"

I blink. She's not letting anything stay unsaid today. "Ending to, um, coming here. Ending my therapy."

Her eyebrow's up, a tiny bit. "*Nice, neat.* Hmm. Tell me, do you think I see you as a case that I'm eager to tie up with a ribbon, nicely, neatly, and put away, mark it closed, success, The End?"

"I don't know."

She breaks into a broad grin. "I assure you, I don't think of you like that. I see your dilemma: You would not be able to take the refresher course in senior life-saving to qualify for the waterfront job. To which you have been looking forward."

It's her job to remember things like that. Nevertheless, I feel grateful. "Yes, that's it, exactly.

"Anyway, we were coming to the Brooklyn Battery Tunnel. When I was little I used to be scared in there. I used to think, What if it starts to leak, what if it caves in on us?

"Mom told me how when you do a survey you mark off sites into grid patterns with little flags. The trouble with those is, the local cows sometimes eat them. So then you have to put more. You can't use wire, because the cows would eat that too, and it would hurt them. She mentioned how many centimeters down you have to dig, and how you sift the soil, and how many artifacts per square meter constitute a potential dig site.

"The roadway started sloping up; we were nearly through. Mom said, 'You'd get a little taste of what it feels like to us archo-jocks, digging up the past.'

"Daylight ahead. We drove out of the tunnel. We came to the tolls. I thought about the fine sandy beach at Silverbirch, and of floating on top of the sparkling weed-free water. On the other hand, North Dakota, rugged, spacious, farther than I've ever traveled. . . . I asked her, 'Mom,' stalling for time, I guess, 'what do you do with the stuff you dig up?'

"She said, 'We try to piece it together. Learn what we can from it.' "

Dr. Schneck says, semi-joking, "Like what we do here."

"Right. I thought of that. As soon as we were past the

tolls, I told Mom about coming to you. I knew from her face it came as a blow, like saying, Yes, ma'am, your daughter has problems. But she was also glad for me. And another feeling I got was that she was thinking maybe *she* should go to somebody. I don't know, maybe I just want her to. Anyhow, she asked me in a quiet voice, 'Dinah, is it helping?'

"We were driving along the East River. A tugboat chugged up it, like Little Toot come to life. Beyond it the miles and miles of factories and warehouses of Williamsburg and Queens somehow looked less bleak and dreary than usual. And to my left all of Manhattan spread out, exciting, glittery. I said, 'Yes, Mom, it's starting to help.'

Hearing myself say those words, *starting to,* I get terrifically sad, thinking, Now that it's ending!

Dr. Schneck smiles placidly. This session is about to end.

"I don't know what I'm going to do," I say in a frazzled voice. "Mom has to let McVeigh know, I have to let her know, before we leave for London. How can I decide? I've got too much else on my mind. Tomorrow Gray's parents arrive, I have to get ready to meet them. Wednesday he graduates, and Thursday he leaves." My voice drops wretchedly low, as the summer stretches before me like a desert—regardless of where I'll be. Dr. Schneck leans forward, straining to hear. I whisper almost inaudibly, "We'll be apart. I won't see him for such a long time."

"You make it sound," says Dr. Schneck, "as though being apart from people has to mean you lose them."

167

I do? I suppose so. Well, why does it mean that to me? Because, when you come down to it, it's true, isn't it? Hey, please, please, Dr. Schneck, don't put your hands on the chair arms just yet! Let's talk about it some more! . . .

She smiles. She stands. I have to leave.

XV

Thursday, May 19, 4:20–5:10 P.M.

I don't want to sit down yet. I hold on to the back of the patient's chair, look around, get a start on good-byes:

To the Levolors, my pals, that keep the outside out of here. To the plants on the plant stand; avocado, you too. To the little cat with the Egyptian smile up on the shelf near the ceiling. To the rug. I shut my eyes. Maize, blue, orange, white, right. I've memorized the thread succession. In a pinch, I can make this rug appear on the insides of my eyelids, all its threads in order.

Good-bye to the end table at the head of the couch; to the glass ashtray that never has any butts in it; and the cream-colored telephone that instead of ringing, tactfully flashes a light so she'll know there's a message for her.

Good-bye to the couch, only non-snail-color furniture item. Do people take their shoes off before they lie down on it? *Lie,* and *lie*—funny that two such different actions have to share one verb. Lying, not lying, on the Futon last night, experiencing that "last" in both senses of the word, and with all my senses. . . . But on this couch, in this room, how would it feel to lie down, facing away from Dr. Schneck? Would the hidden-away things float more easily into awareness? And what about the count- less wisps and fragments, untranslatable into words, that always flit through people's minds? Is the upholstery fabric of this couch sea-blue-green on purpose, so that the wisps and fragments might undergo a sea change, be- come possible to say?

"Won't you sit down?" she says.

I sit. "I've been putting it off, because it's for the last time."

She blithely asks me, "Why?"

Hey, she can't have turned senile on me between Monday and now! "Because," I say extra-patiently— extra-patiently, huh? There's another double-edged word, words are having their fun with me. . . . "Be- cause, as you know, this is my last session."

She nods, looks entirely placid.

"Four hours from now I'll be on the plane to London. I feel ridiculous sitting here! Other people would be rushing around, doing last-minute errands, would make sure they've packed everything. Not too many would be at a therapy session. Especially not their last."

"*Ridiculous?* How? I don't quite see."

"Well, I rushed here, all eager, didn't want to miss a minute of it. I *needed* to come. I shouldn't need it so badly now that I'm supposed to be done."

" 'Supposed to be done'?" she muses.

"I know why you're smiling. You think it sounds like a three-minute egg, or a roast leg of lamb!" I mimic the sound the timer on our stove makes when something's ready.

"You make it sound like that," she says with a broader smile.

"It's not a joke. Anyway, I can't worry about it. There's too much else I have to get said. So much, I don't know where to start."

She opens her hands in her lap, meaning, wherever I start is okay.

I study how she does that. I open *my* hands. I'll have to make that gesture to myself from now on. Will it do me any good?

Okay, I start with Lucky. "They did the bypass on Monday. It went really well. He can already walk on the leg. And he's been good about not smoking. The doctor's optimistic. Joe's elated, as you can imagine.

"Joe graduated, no hitch. And Gray got an award. And Beauty's doing just great. There was a lot to celebrate, so we had a party. Yesterday, graduation day, late. After Joe's and Gray's parents went back, to Chicago and to Naples. It really took off. The party, I mean. But

I'm skipping around. Wait, I'll tell you about the award.

"Tuesday, Class Day, I sat with Gray's parents. The graduates were on the stage of the new gym. His father makes me so uncomfortable! He's big and broad, handsome in a macho way, with a beer belly that he acts proud of. I don't mean to put him down. I really tried to like him. He didn't give me a chance. He kept talking down New York, and New Yorkers. He acted like I was a wise-ass snob who'd look down on small-town people, consider them hicks.

"Mrs. Dawson appealed to me more. I guess I was ready to like her because there's a lot of Gray in her features. I felt bad for her, too. She was even more uncomfortable than I was, helpless-seeming, shy, apologetic. Tuesday was a warm, sticky day. She sweated through her polyester blouse and suit jacket; her armpits were drenched. Her skirt was too tight; she kept tugging at it. And she had a new permanent, too curly and frizzy.

"The one time I saw her get happy—me too, we were equally surprised—was when the Dean of Students called 'Graham Hopkins Dawson.' Hopkins is her maiden name, by the way. Gray was surprised himself. He hadn't even known there was such a thing as the Kenneth T. Burkhalter Prize for Outstanding Achievement in Biology.

"I wish Gray could have seen his father's face. That one moment his father looked proud and pleased. The rest of the time he had a big chip on his shoulder.

"Something else happened during Class Day, before the speeches and awards. Mrs. Donadio was there—her son's in the graduating class—and she came over to me, all excited. No, this is off the subject. It'll throw me off the track.

"Gray's parents stayed at the Hilton. Tuesday night they took us to one of the restaurants there. Pretentious, snotty waiters, menus in French, cynical prices. It added fuel to Mr. Dawson's complaints about New York. Gray said it wasn't a typical restaurant, which made things worse, because Mr. Dawson had chosen it.

"He had such an edge to him! Every remark out of him was a reproach to Gray for not being like Todd, the *good* son, for refusing to devote his entire future to Dawson Construction. He'll have a rough summer down there.

"Gray's mom just sat helplessly through it. Gray tried to justify himself, didn't get anywhere, quit, ate in silence. I chattered away, over-eager, just to keep things going. I told about the birth of Beauty, Gray's bravery and presence of mind. 'You ought to go down there and see her; she's really something. And you'll get a big welcome; they'll roll out the red carpet for you.' What feeble pleasantry.

" 'I wish we could,' Mrs. Dawson started to say. But Mr. Dawson said they wouldn't have time, had to get on the plane home right after graduation.

"The party last night"—*all* of last night, except Julie's drunk scene—"was great. Wine, beer, popcorn, pizza, no big preparations. Just the right music, just the right people.

"Julie wore her new Laura Ashley dress, demurely bare and sexy. She started out in a glow of self-confidence about having lost ten pounds finally. She hadn't eaten dinner, though, and drank a lot on an empty stomach.

"Half the party was in Joe's room. He was playing the piano in there, getting a lot of sound out of it, considering it's a tinny old upright. It was kind of a debut for him. He'd never played anything but records before when there were people other than Gray and me present. He warmed up with some standard tunes, then started improvising. It sounded really good. The music kept changing, from wistful longing, to teasing, bouncy, and got boisterous when you least expected it. At one point he did variations on a tantalizing melody I couldn't place at first. Oh, right, Lucky's 'Bypass Rag.' Only Joe'd transposed, transformed it from sardonic and brooding to rambunctious and fun.

"In the middle of it Julie waltzed, no, wobbled in and tripped, luckily right in front of me. I caught her before she fell.

"I maneuvered her over to the window seat, threw the window open. 'Come on, Julie, let's sit here a couple of minutes together.'

" '*Together*, that's a good one! *You* may be together. Well, not me! I just guzzled a few thousand calories; all my weight'll creep back on; the scale'll scream at me in the morning, and so will my mother; I'll be hung over all the way to L.A.' She put her head in my lap, told me she was scared that she wouldn't measure up out there, wished she weren't going, hiccuped loudly. Then she counted up all the therapists she's ever been to. 'And I told you all their names. And you've been holding out on me, you've only gone to one, and haven't told me her name. Come on, Dinah, who's your shrink?'

"It's true, I didn't want to before. I didn't feel right about it. Last night I went ahead and told her, and felt okay about it."

"Good," says Dr. Schneck. She's pleased.

"Julie went to sleep. Or passed out, I don't know which. When people left, she woke up, was okay, and Joe took her home.

"This next part I don't know if I should tell you."

"Why not?"

"Gray and me, our last time. It has to last . . ." Still another sense of the word! "It has to last me the whole summer."

"And you think telling about it will diminish it?"

"No, I guess not. Not if I can do it justice. But . . ." I look at her wrinkled cheeks, her wrinkled neck. "I know I'm not supposed to worry about this, but are you sure it won't make you feel bad?"

"You mean, because I am not young? Because you think such nights may not be part of my life now?" A brightness comes into her voice that I treasure. "Yes, I am absolutely sure."

"Gray left this morning in a rented U-Haul with all his stuff, except his phonograph, which he's leaving for Joe, and two of his posters, the roseate spoonbill and the manatee; I'm keeping those. Last night, after the party, though, all the animal posters were still on the walls, and the Futon was still on the floor.

"I gave him his farewell present. I'd gotten the idea

for it on the drive back from Mom's last week: a great new recording of Haydn's *Creation*, the same one we heard on the radio in the car.

"We lay in each other's arms and listened to it. Wait, I have to tell you something, going back to Easter Sunday night, that time at the stables: You were right. When I took a chance on getting pregnant, I *was* trying to prove something, answering Mom: See, Mom, this is how serious I am about Gray.

"Last night . . . well, last night was better. I had the diaphragm in. It bothers me when I think about it. I stopped thinking about it. Outside noises stopped. Time stopped. All there was was feeling. So much, I thought I couldn't bear it. But then I stopped thinking even that. Here's what remained: Us turning into our whole selves, no division between what we did with our bodies and what was happening in our psyches, souls, whatever you call it. Phew! I'm entangled in words. I can see why some novels skip right to 'afterward.' For 'during' you have to invent new words, like Adam and Eve had to, when they named things in Eden. Because if you use the words there already are—four-letter, fancy, or both kinds—it makes it commonplace, just something everybody does. But while it's 'during,' when it's right, you're the only ones, the whole thing exists only in you and through you and for you. I mean, us. That's how it felt. Except, these words *do* apply—"

"Yes? What are they?"

"Making love. We made love. I couldn't ever say it, before."

"I know. I'm happy that you can, now."

176

I ask, "Do you think it's because of therapy?" Before she can ask me back, as I know she will, Do *I* think so, I say, "*I* think it is. That's saying a lot more than what I told Mom, that this is *starting* to help. It's saying"—I look right into Dr. Schneck's eyes—"I've come a long way."

Now I should feel great. But the words boomerang back in my face. A long way—right! Gray's gone many hundred miles by now, is driving through where— South Carolina? Georgia? And in a few hours *I'll* be a few thousand miles away, from him, from here. "I feel awful! I'm doing a tailspin, I'm scared, I'm ashamed! I've talked myself blue in the face, blue all through. I rushed to get I don't know where to, into this total funk. How'll I get out of it? I've talked away this whole session, and don't even know what I'll tell Mom! I'm torn! I *want* to go to North Dakota; I don't want to tell her no, but I can't see giving up Silverbirch. I can't be that much better, can I, if I'm carrying on like this. Excuse me." I reach for a Kleenex and bawl like a baby. "What a way of ending therapy!"

She leans forward. "You also feel torn about, as you say, 'ending therapy.' You put off sitting down, remember? Because it was for 'the last time.' You looked around the room as if you wanted to memorize it. You told me how much you needed this session, more than one should need a 'last' session. The word *last* came up many times.

"As for the question of how far you've come, and whether you are better, you told me eloquently, and I was moved to hear, how you have opened yourself to feelings. You can feel love. You can make it, beautifully, and call it by its name. The 'tailspin' you then went into is very understandable. You took back, at least momentarily, that you've changed—so that I won't let you go."

"No, that's wrong." I want to think, There she goes, making herself important, as if she were somebody in my life. No use. I can't deny it: She *is* somebody to me. "*I'*m the one who's going! On this trip with Dad and Audrey, I have to. Then either out to North Dakota with Mom, or to Silverbirch. Then it'll be fall, and I'll go to Florida, to be with Gray. So it isn't *you* letting *me* go." This last part I emphasize, but do not believe.

She smiles. She knows. She's on to this. "Yes, I'm aware of your plans. You have learned many things about yourself, including that partings are scary to you, and plans can be reassuring. Of course there is a great deal still to be learned. You may want at some time—" right at the moment I both want, and don't want, to hear this—"to resume therapy. I've enjoyed very much working with you. I would be glad to see you anytime. Things need not go badly, you know, for you to want to resume. I certainly hope you will come in when you can, and let me know what is happening with you."

"Okay, I guess I'm glad you said that; I just can't think about it now. I'm trying to think what to tell Mom."

She sits back and says, "What comes to your mind?" as though there was a whole bunch of time, instead of just a minute, left.

178

Two things: My first session, how I kept saying I was just here that one time, just to please my father.

The other thing I tell her: "Mrs. Donadio told me, on Class Day—she was all excited about it—Isabelle Markson has just agreed to give a poetry course next fall. She's my favorite poet. It's ironic. It's so unfair! Why couldn't Gray and I have met at that course instead of Zankow's? I don't know why I should be thinking of a thing like that at a time like this!"

Hands hovering over her chair arms.

"I'll think about you a lot, Dr. Schneck."

"I'll think about you, Dinah."

We both stand. I'm startled by how short she is. She has to tilt her small, green-eyed, broad-nosed, wide-mouthed, big-eared wrinkled face up, for us to smile at each other.

She holds her hand out. You'd think that nobody, not even I, could misread the simple gesture. Well, I think it's to open the door for me. I want to save her the trouble, so I open it myself, and I start to go through. Then I turned around, though, and I realize it wasn't that at all!

It was to shake hands. We do. And wish each other a good summer.

* * * * *

It's Friday afternoon, my first week back at Barnard.
I'm sitting on the same Leatherette stool, facing the back
wall with the mirror to the right. There's a big turn-
over in personnel here. Amazingly, though, my counterman is George. Gray would get a kick out of that. When
I get home, I'll call him up, what the hell, make the
phone company still a little richer. We already made
their summer extra-profitable, calling each other long
distance at least every other day.

I came here straight from English 353x, Isabelle
Markson's course. She's middle-aged, heavy in the
bosom, thick in the waist, brown hair, brown eyes,

180

freckled face, plain as a wren. Nothing "poetic" about her. She doesn't act "distinguished" either. But she *is*.

There are only twenty-three people in the class. That's because you had to submit samples of your work. Not necessarily finished poems. "Work in progress" was okay.

I had two things I thought I might submit.

One was "To Fargo." I started it on the plane to North Dakota. Flying gives me a terrific high. The poem —I didn't even know it was going to be one—just came spilling out. It was as if the words took over; all I had to do was let them. The title words played games with me: Too Far to Go to Fargo? Or, to Forego to Go to Fargo? I was glad I was going. What I forewent, if there is such a word, was the refresher course in lifesaving— but I *was* saving a part of my life. And I forewent the waterfront job. But not my whole Silverbirch summer. They gave me back my old counselor job, and that was not so bad. *Foregone,* in the other sense also, also got into the poem "in progress" in the air: Things from before, that were gone, or at least seemed to be gone. A lot of hopes went into it, too—which mostly came true. My three weeks on the survey didn't make an archo-jock out of me. The artifacts that turned up were mostly flakes of Knife River Flint, everyday stuff to the experts. But Mom and I got along, and pieced together a few fargone things we thought we had both foregone.

The second poem "in progress" is "Skunk Song." I started it in a letter to Gray. I made the skunk a female. She's piling up leaves with her forepaws. She envisions the home she is building, and sings from inside her skunk self about her skunk lover/mate. I used mainly clipped, staccato words, to give it a chattery sound. I tried for creature-ishness. And it's mysterious, especially the parts where I didn't know what I was doing.

I couldn't decide for the longest time which to send. I didn't know if there was any point to sending one, because my plans for the fall were up in the air, so to speak.

All summer I thought about "apart," and how, and if, it's related to losing.

I missed Gray terribly. I do now. Bodily, with my whole self. "As bad as a pig up a tree would miss slop," as he so poetically put it the morning we stood on 111th Street and Amsterdam Avenue hugging and kissing, before he climbed into the U-Haul and drove on down to Naples, Florida. But we wrote each other a few hundred letters, talked on the phone, and we didn't come apart—yet. I know I have to add "yet." Because we still might. Any two people might. Risking love is scary. There are no guarantees.

One morning I woke up and I knew just what to do: What the hell, send both poems "in progress."

Isabelle Markson wrote these comments in the margins: *"Inventive." "Original."* Also, *"Still too vague." "What do you mean here?" "Work on this part some more."* Attached was a note: *"Very promising. I hope to see you in my class."*

It was the opposite of Zankow's. She asked people to name poems they either liked or disliked a lot. Not to show up anyone's poor taste or make anyone feel dumb. To help her structure the course, and to get more than a quick first impression of what sort of people we are. A feeling sprang up of all of us being colleagues. That's very rare in a classroom. I wish Gray could have been there.

Joe waited for me after class. Not by coincidence. I'd told him I'd be there.

He put off law school till next year, or longer, or for good, if he makes it as a musician. He's giving himself this year to try. He already has two jobs: One at WNYC, "entry level," meaning man of all work, mainly in the mail room, but with a chance to produce some of their jazz shows later on. The other job is as gofer/ Man Friday for the Curtis Montgomery Trio, newly formed, already with quite a few gigs lined up. Lucky is the pianist. They can't pay Joe much in cash. But the deal includes the spare room in Lucky's apartment, formal piano lessons, and a chance to become their manager if the trio is a success.

He wanted me to go check out the place, see where he'd be living.

"I'd like to, Joe. Just not right now."

"Why not? Where are you going?"

"Over to Chock Full o' Nuts."

You don't have to explain things to him. He realized what day it was. Exactly a year ago I met Gray. Joe, too, for that matter. He blinked his big dark melting eyes and kidded, as to Greta Garbo of old, "You vant to be alone. Okay, see you later."

I sip my commemorative coffee, ask if I can have a doughnut, to make it as close to last year as I can.

Here's how this year shapes up: I threw out the pro-

183

gram Mrs. Donadio made me fill out that day in her office. I'm taking Markson's course, Shakespeare, American History, and—out of curiosity—Psychoanalytic Approaches to Literature. I don't have to declare a major till spring, but I already know: English, emphasis on writing.

And I'm planning to move. Dad agrees I should be nearer to school. I'm Number 383 on the waiting list for Barnard-approved housing, so it may take a while.

Julie's back, Joe's back; I have my other friends, and there'll be new ones, of course. Still, as Joe said, I'm alone. That's okay; I'm counting the days till Columbus Day weekend. I'll either go down to Florida or Gray'll come up here. Unless he comes sooner, which he said he might do if they give him a weekend off.

I trace the raised spine of my silver bracelet, touch the tiny thorns on the stems of the roses.

Enough commemoration. Time to go home. I pick up my books. Hey, a déjà vu. That's when you think you see something you've seen before, sometime in the past. I've been reading about things like that. It's interesting. When I go see Dr. Schneck—I mean to, one of these days—I'll tell her about it.

The counterman, George, is holding his chin in his hand and he says, "I've worked in this joint too long! Now I'm one of the nuts in the chock! Say, you two, haven't you done this same routine before?"

There's a rose, deep red, lying (but it's true!) on my doughnut.

"I"—(Ah)—"just got too lonesome, so I flew on up. I kind of hoped I'd be in time for that class you wrote me about. I missed it by just a few minutes. So then I had a hunch I just might find you in here."

We're in each other's arms. *In the language of kisses* —that'll be the name of a poem I may start, next time I'm in an airplane.

Right now I'm living it.

Afterward there's the whole weekend! And Joe still has the apartment, and if he's not home when we go there, that's okay; Gray still has the key.

---

*   *   *   *   *

Doris Orgel

is the award-winning, highly acclaimed author of many books, including two for Dial, *The Devil in Vienna* and *A Certain Magic,* both of which were ALA Notable Books. In a starred review *Booklist* applauded *The Devil in Vienna* as "A poignant story of love and loss. . . . Orgel's sure focus allows her to draw in a large assortment of character and incident with rich and very real effects."

She was born in Vienna, Austria, and lived there until Hitler came to power and her family managed to escape, first to Yugoslavia and then to England. Mrs. Orgel now lives in New York City.